Death
Rattles

ANDY RAUSCH

Burning Bulb
PUBLISHING

Death Rattles
By **Andy Rausch**

Burning Bulb Publishing
P.O. Box 4721
Bridgeport, WV 26330-4721
United States of America
www.BurningBulbPublishing.com

Cover designed by Gary Lee Vincent with the following licensed elements from Can Stock Photo, Inc.: csp19832874

First Edition.

Paperback Edition ISBN: 978-0692264720

Printed in the United States of America

This collection is dedicated to its spiritual father, Stephen King, as well as my wife, Kerri, to whom everything I write is dedicated.

"Where there is no imagination, there is no horror."
—Arthur Conan Doyle

"Wop-bop-a-lu-bop-ba-bop-bam-boom!"
—Little Richard

CONTENTS

INTRODUCTION

The short story format is said to have originated in the Seventeenth century in the form of oral storytelling. While subject matter of these early stories probably varied from accounts of powerful gods, legendary acts of human heroics, and deadly battles with fierce beasts, no doubt Seventeenth century man also crafted a horrific tale or two in the hopes of scaring the living shit out of his pals. And thus the horror short story was born.

Now skip way ahead to 1983 where ten-year-old me is staying up way past my bedtime to sneak a peek at episodes of *The Twilight Zone* and *Alfred Hitchcock Presents* with host "Uncle" Ed Muscari on Kansas City's KSHB-TV. You see, I had this trick where I would close my door, turn down the TV to where it was barely audible, and then tuck a blanket under the crack of the door so no one could see the light of my tiny black-and-white TV. Episodes of those old television series would serve as my earliest introduction to the horror short story. That led to my tracking down those old Gold Key *Twilight Zone* comic books, which in turn led me to eventually discover old E.C. comics like *Tales from the Crypt* and *Vault of Horror*, as well as Warren Publishing books *Creepy* and *Eerie*.

It was around this same time I came across my first collection of short stories by Edgar Allan Poe. Between the pages of that book I soon discovered worlds of terror I had thus far been unfamiliar with. I read *The Cask of Amontillado*. And *The Gold Bug*. *The Tell-Tale Heart*. *Masque of the Red Death*. As it turned out, this Poe guy was pretty fucking good. Between the introductions of Poe and *The Twilight Zone's* Rod Serling, I knew then I wanted to be a writer. I mean, what was there not to love? These were two men who were literally drunk on the power of creation. (Poe was apparently

1

drunk and high on other substances, as well, but that's a discussion for another day...)

Around this same time I started watching something called *Creature Feature*. The show, also on KSHB-TV, was hosted by a portly Vampira-wannabe who called herself Crematia Mortem. The show featured old cornball "B" horror movies, and these had a huge impact on my ideas of what horror was. I remember there was one movie called *Sssssss* starring Strother Martin that came on every couple of months. In that film, a character was slowly transformed into a cobra snake (and is ultimately killed by a mongoose). This was respectable highbrow stuff to be sure! But nevertheless, crappy horror pictures such as these would prove to be a huge influence on me.

It wasn't until I was in the sixth grade, however, that I stumbled across the author who would prove to be my greatest revelation regarding the horror genre. The book was called *Carrie*, and it had been written by this guy named Stephen King. Turned out this Stephen King guy was pretty fucking good, too! I was a bit of an outsider at school, so this tale of one oddball's telekinetic vengeance against her peers resonated quite a bit with me. Soon I was reading every King book I could get my grubby little paws on. I remember being so frightened by King's graphic description of the undead Victor Pascow in *Pet Sematary* that I shelved that book at once and vowed never to finish it. Then I woke up in the wee hours that night and could practically hear the book calling to me. So I gave in, got the damned book down, and finished it all in that single sitting.

But as much as I loved King's early full-length efforts (still my favorites of his) like *'Salem's Lot*, *The Shining*, *Cujo*, *The Stand*, etc., I found myself truly in love with the man once I discovered his short stories collected in the anthologies *Night Shift* and *Skeleton Crew*. These stories, originally published in nudie mags like *Cavalier* and *Hustler*, would forever change my perception of what horror could be. These stories—much like the ones in this volume—weren't limited to traditional horror, but King used the trappings of the genre to frame these exotic tales.

Looking over my own stories, I now see that some of King's lesser works were often the biggest influences on my own work. Take for instance King's tale *The Boogeyman*, in which a psychiatrist ultimately reveals himself to be the Boogeyman wearing a psychiatrist mask... Or *Battleground*, which told the story of tiny toy soldiers doing battle with a full-sized human killer... Or *Trucks*, which later served as the inspiration for King's film *Maximum Overdrive*, and painted a picture of automobiles and appliances, come to life... Or *Survivor Type*, in which a stranded man slowly eats himself (literally) to death... Surely no one would point at these stories and claim them to be King's finest work, and yet they are stunning (and beautiful, in their way) if only for their sheer audacity and balls-out creativity. They may not be King's strongest works, but they are certainly among his most enjoyable.

So I guess all this is to warn you that these stories aren't anything complex and profound like King's *The Stand*, but rather, something more akin to the simple pleasures of *Sometimes They Come Back* or *The Ledge* or even *Old Chief Woodenhead*. And, be they good or bad in your estimation, I don't want to give the credit (or blame, as it were) to King. The stories in this collection are mine. Stephen King was their primary influence, sure, but I was their creator.

These aren't all horror stories, either, but each and every tale here is part of a darker world where things aren't always what they appear to be. The world of this book is a place where ghosts and goblins lurk within the shadows, vengeance is always around the corner, and anything can and will happen. In fact, the more ridiculous the scenario, the more likely it is to appear within these pages.

I think it was Alexander Payne, the film director, who once told me that he didn't believe we ever really know who our primary influences are. He said something like, "I know who and what I *want* my primary influences to be, but that isn't always the way it works." But that is not the case here. While I might also like to credit the likes of Elmore Leonard, Ray Bradbury, Clive Barker, Kurt Vonnegut, Richard Matheson, Poe, and the aforementioned comics, TV shows, and movies as inspirations, I think King's influence is the most prevalent in my short stories.

This is not to say I write like Stephen King. Not at all. That would be a grandiose statement for any writer to make. This is not to say I wouldn't *like* to write like King, or Matheson, or Barker, but I think the author I write most like is Andy Rausch. And hopefully, after you've read this volume, you'll say Andy Rausch is pretty fucking good, too!

—Andy Rausch

MY BELOVED ROSIE

My beloved Rosie was dying and there wasn't a damned thing I could do about it. We'd been married for fifty-eight years and I had vowed to take care of her, in sickness and in health. But what of the things I couldn't control? What of this damnable cancer that now ravaged her body and promised to take her away from me at any given moment? I know it was ridiculous because there was nothing I could possibly do about any of it, but I felt like a failure. I felt like I was letting down my beloved Rosie because I couldn't snap my fingers and somehow make her pain go away.

Yes, she was dying and there was nothing to be done. And while I'm sure the knowledge of her impending departure bothered her far more than she let on, there was no doubt she was handling it better than I. She had her great god in the sky to look up to, and she believed in death being the gateway to a better place. I did not. I've never called myself an atheist or agnostic or whatever other labels might apply, namely because I've never taken the time to examine my own beliefs, or lack thereof, under any sort of microscope. I just found all religion to be horse shit, a sort of man-made escapism from the terrible realities of a finite life. And that stance had served me just fine—until now. Now I longed to have Rosie's belief in a better tomorrow. I felt as if I could somehow convince myself that the good are rewarded with heaven, I could somehow come to grips with this awful predicament.

Of course I couldn't convince myself of something I just outright didn't believe in. I could no more convince myself that some benevolent sky-wizard reigned over all of us, looking to reward our good deeds and punish us for being bad, than I could that the earth was flat or Vietnam had been a

4

good idea. It just couldn't be done. So here I was, stuck in my own misery with the knowledge that my beloved had less than two months to live.

And if she died, then what? What would happen to *me*? Surely I, too, would succumb to death as I couldn't imagine any sort of life, meaningful or otherwise, without Rosie. She was more than the light of my life—she was my life in totality. She was my reason for living. She was, as the song says, my first, my last, my everything. I felt we were intertwined, one in the same, and that one could not survive without the other. Perhaps she would have been strong enough to go on without me, but I certainly had no chance of making it without her.

So that was that. I had less than two months to accept the fact that mine and Rosie's lives—together and perhaps singularly apart—were about to come to an abrupt halt. And if Rosie died and I lived, then perhaps, I thought, I would do a Hemingway and take my own life. I knew just how I'd do it... I'd go out into our living room, surrounded by all our memories, and put a shotgun in my mouth. And then I would pull the trigger and be gone, not to meet my beloved Rosie or sit at the feet of some god, but to nothing at all; nothing more than blackness and silence.

And that was fine by me, for I could imagine nothing more.

Rosie was in bad shape these days. Her arthritis had become almost too much for her to bear, and she couldn't even tend to the garden she so loved. I had always hated gardening, but now I found myself taking care of the damn thing in her stead, doing whatever I could to make her remaining time as pleasant as possible. And, to Rosie's credit, she appreciated my efforts, as haphazard as they might have been. I knew about as much about gardening as I did god. And the garden itself was no help; it had never been much for growing things, but Rosie had somehow managed to make those tomatoes sprout up from that stale earth through something like sheer will.

As I said, I myself, I never cared much for gardening. I preferred hobbies which gave me pleasure, and gardening certainly did not, save for watching that smile creep across Rosie's face. My hobbies had been reading trashy detective novels, cheering on my Detroit Tigers in the summer, and listening to old Beach Boys records. But none of these was my primary past-time; no, that designation was reserved for loving Rosie. As I've said, she had always been my everything, and I couldn't imagine an existence without her in it. We'd met when we were eighteen, and I'd spent just about every day since with her, barring military service or unforeseeable acts of nature.

Now each day was the same, running together in a blur with an ever-increasing speed that neither of us could slow, life racing towards death. I would be there in the garden with my old straw farmer's hat on to block the sun, my sleeves rolled up, a bandana around my neck for sweat, and Rosie would be sitting in her rocker up on the porch, knitting. We would listen to the radio. Sometimes we listened to my Tigers, and Rosie was a good sport when we did. She would comment on the progress of players and the season, pretending for my benefit to care. She would clap and cheer in a delightfully silly manner (which I adored) every time the Tigers got a hit. But most of the time we listened to her music—she especially loved Herb Alpert and his Tijuana Brass—and that seemed to keep her in good spirits. She never insisted that we listen to her music, and I certainly never protested it; the woman would be dead and gone before baseball season was over, so I figured I'd do whatever I could to let her enjoy the last of her time.

It was a Tuesday night, about three a.m., and I couldn't sleep. I rarely sleep now, so I suppose the specific day of the week was a moot point. It's not so much that I have nightmares as I just find myself staring intently at Rosie, deep in her sleep, looking peaceful as ever, appearing as young and vibrant as she ever had. So I got up to fix myself a glass of milk and I sat down in the kitchen to read the newspaper, just as I had on so many other sleepless nights.

I scanned the front of the newspaper and found nothing new there; one political party was calling the other party a failure, and neither of them was doing anything much to try and change anything beyond public opinion. I turned the page to the obituaries, which were, at my age, like a sad reunion with long-forgotten friends, coworkers, and loved ones. I read through a couple of entries—nothing much out of the ordinary—and then I happened to notice one in particular. The woman's name was Dorothy Kashyck. I didn't know her, but I knew that last name well. I quickly scanned through the woman's obit, finally finding what I was looking for; amongst the survivors was a man named Darnell Kashyck.

Just seeing the name brought back a million memories.

Darnell Kashyck.

Yes, Darnell Kashyck, the man who had raped my Rosie...

He was still alive. He was older than I; I figured him for about eighty, eighty-one.

And the wheels started to turn.

My beloved Rosie had been as pure as the driven snow when we'd met, but she had already been deflowered. Her previous boyfriend, one Darnell Kashyck, had seen to that when he'd held her down and raped her in his garage, his hand clasped over her mouth. She'd clawed and scraped at his face, leaving some damage there, but she'd never told anyone what he'd done to her for fear that she'd be ridiculed and forced to relive the traumatic struggle.

But she told me.

She told me the night before we were married, and I wept. She said she told me so I could reconsider marrying her if I liked. Of course that was never an option for me. My heart was heavy and my body hurt throughout, but it wasn't pain for myself—it was pain for Rosie. I would have done anything for her, and I wanted so badly then to avenge the theft of her purity, but I had been strong enough to resist.

I had been a strong man back then.

I finished what was left of my milk and went back to bed, now lying there awake for a completely different reason. Just as I had before, I found myself staring at Rosie, lost in slumber. But now my thoughts were of a different nature. Now I wasn't thinking so much about my wife's impending death as I was that incident which had occurred to her some sixty years before.

I wondered if Rosie still thought about it. Now, fifty-eight years into our perfect life, was there any need to reflect upon such injustices? Or, even more to the point, would Rosie have any choice in the matter of whether or not she thought back upon the incident? I tried redirection, telling myself that Rosie had surely stopped looking back. After all, she had stopped crying and screaming out in her sleep some thirty years ago.

But how could I have ever let Darnell Kashyck go on living his ordinary life? He had had a wife and children and a successful job of some sort, and Rosie had been forced to remain silent and suppress her pain.

And now, all these years later, I found myself unable to breathe.

And I didn't want to—not if it meant breathing the same air as Kashyck.

And I knew at once what had to be done.

I couldn't control Rosie's cancer. I couldn't control her arthritis. I couldn't hold back the blanket of death that would cover her soon enough.

But here was something I could do.

I could kill Darnell Kashyck.

I waited several days before taking the twenty mile trek out to Edinborough, where Kashyck lived. I'd told Rosie I was going out to look at lawnmowers at the farm store. I didn't want her to know I was visiting Kashyck. I didn't want her to worry, and I wouldn't have wanted to remind her of the man's awful deed. Besides, she and her benevolent god wouldn't have approved of such a thing. But hell, even the Good Book had that bit about an eye for an eye. I knew that was out of context, but I gladly accepted it as all the endorsement I needed to avenge my Rosie. If her god was fine with it, then Rosie herself would have no choice but to go along with the thing. I knew this was faulty logic, and I knew my Rosie would never have signed off on this, but I figured sometimes people, in this case Rosie, just couldn't see what was in their best interests.

But I could see it clearly.

It was about ten-thirty in the morning, a nice, warm, sunny day, when I went to see Darnell Kashyck. His house was easy enough to find, located right smack dab in the middle of a picturesque neighborhood filled with bright, rainbow-hued houses. Kashyck's place was old and rundown, at odds with the rest of the neighborhood. I parked the old Buick at the curb, right in front of Kashyck's mailbox, and made my way up the walkway.

I rang the doorbell, but the thing was dead. So I knocked, but there was no movement inside. I waited a moment and I knocked again, just a bit harder this time, and I could hear grumbling from within the house. "Hold on, hold on," came the old man's voice. "I'll be right there."

And the door opened.

And there he was—Darnell Kashyck, an older version of the man who had taken Rosie's purity, but clearly the same man. He was feeble, bald now, his skin thin and wrinkled with liver spots, and he was wearing an oxygen tube in his nose. He moved with a walker. There was a strange, far off look in his eyes... What was it? Was he lost? Crazed? All of the above?

Kashyck opened the screen door and said, "Thank goodness you're here, Ernie."

And my heart sunk a little.

He called me Ernie again, and I knew my revenge had come too late. Kashyck was now a man of diminished mental ability, lost in dementia. He let me in the house, calling me Ernie as he did, and I entered. Not thinking about my own safety, but operating out of sheer instinct, I turned and scanned the street to make sure I hadn't been seen. I saw no one, and I closed the door behind me.

Kashyck smiled a toothless grin and told me his Evelyn would be home in a bit. I had done my research prior to my visit, and I knew that his wife, Evelyn, had been dead for a decade now. But here he was, this poor, deluded shell of a man, still waiting for his wife and Ernie, probably dead, as well, to come and visit.

I felt sorry for him, thanking the stars I had not fallen victim to this condition. And then, almost as instantly as the feeling of empathy had come, came something else—a new emotion I didn't recognize at first... And my mood darkened. I now realized that this new emotion was a rage-fueled hatred. Hatred for this man who had hurt my Rosie, and an even more powerful hatred for his condition which had beaten me to my revenge.

Kashyck said something about Ronald Reagan, as if the man was still alive and still in office. I now realized that he and I were a lot alike at this moment—he was here, trapped in the Eighties, and I was here, trapped in the time so long ago when he'd raped my Rosie.

"My hip hurts, Ernie," Kashyck said, turning towards me. And then he asked, "What time will Mommy and Daddy be home tonight?"

I was stunned and confused, but my body knew exactly what to do. I was running on auto-pilot now. As Kashyck continued to ramble on about his parents, and Ernie, and his hip, and Walter Mondale, and so many other things from the past, my hand, without my knowledge, slid down towards my belt. And it went further, until my fingers were caressing the gold handle of that big U.S. Marine Corps commemorative Bowie knife Rosie had once bought me for Christmas.

And as soon as I realized my hand was touching that knife, it was out of its sheath, extended before me, its blade glinting in what little light there was. And again, just as I realized this was happening, my hand shot forward and slashed at Kashyck's abdomen. Blood appeared at once.

Kashyck looked lost. "Ernie?" he asked. "What's wrong, Ernie?"

And my hand was moving again, slashing at Kashyck's chest, catching the dangling oxygen tube, slicing through it.

I felt a vague pang of repulsion at what I had done.

What I was doing.

But it was too late to stop.

Things were already far into motion, moving faster and faster towards the inevitable.

Kashyck stumbled a bit, falling hard to the floor. As I readied that old Bowie knife, Kashyck looked up at me with an expression that was at once that of a sad old man and that of a scared and confused child. A tear rose in Kashyck's eye, wavering there for eternity.

"Ernie," he said. "What time will Mommy and Daddy be home? I'm scared."

And with that, as though his words were some sort of trigger, the knife shot forward and slit his throat. Kashyck reached up towards the wound, falling back down limply, a grotesque gurgling sound coming from within his throat.

And Darnell Kashyck was no more.

Rosie and I were sitting in the back yard in our lawn chairs, listening to the Tigers. They were beating the Royals three to one in the third. Rosie was fumbling with her knitting, accomplishing what little her arthritis would allow. I had just finished my day's work in the garden, and was wiping the sweat from my brow when the local radio station interrupted the commercial break to share some news.

"Eighty-one-year-old Darnell Kashyck of Edinborough is still missing after twenty-two days," the newsman announced. "Police are still investigating the man's disappearance, and now believe that Kashyck, who was of questionable mental health, may have wandered into the nearby woods and gotten lost there..."

Upon hearing that name from so long ago, Rosie cocked her head like a dog hearing a high-pitched sound. She then turned her gaze to the garden, where the tomatoes were growing bigger and more prosperous than they ever had before. I watched for a second as a knowing smile crept across her lips.

"You know," Rosie said, "I've never seen the garden so rich and alive."

And that was all she said.

She took my hand in hers and squeezed it tightly, and we both basked in the warm afternoon sun, living fully in this moment in which we were eternal.

THE $10,000 JOHN WAYNE MAGNUM OPUS

Edison Mayhew was sitting in a corner booth in Bob's Pizza Palace, chatting up an actor over all-you-can-eat pizza buffet. He was paying for the meal, so he got to explain the project to the actor, Jimmy Donovan. Jimmy was hot shit at the moment as he had just appeared in the TV movie *B-Lizzard*, about giant reptiles that attacked and ate people during a snowstorm.

"This movie's gonna be the fourth installment in my *Titty Zombies* series," said Edison. "Have you seen the other three?"

"Well, I've seen one of them," Jimmy said. "I think it was *Titty Zombies 2.*"

"*A Tale of Two Titties*. That's my favorite in the series," said Edison. "Until now."

"Why now?"

Edison smiled proudly. "Because this one's gonna be my greatest film ever. My magnum opus."

"What's the budget?"

"We got $10,000."

"What would my role be?"

"Your role would be Miles Macklemore, a private eye with a taste for broads."

"So this is *noir*?"

"Not really, but it's going to have some *noir* flavor to it."

"And the film, it's guaranteed distribution?"

"Yes, sir," said Edison. "Bloody Mess Pictures made a fortune off the first three, and they've committed to putting out a fourth one."

Jimmy nodded. "What would I get paid?"

"Two hundred and fifty dollars."

"How many days?"

"We would shoot you out in two days."

"And the role, is it a lead?"

Edison squirmed. "Not exactly. But here comes the reason you're gonna wanna make this movie..."

"Okay."

"You'll be the second lead."

"Who's gonna be first?"

"I'm getting to that," said Edison. "Rule number one of no-budget filmmaking is to either have a 'name' actor in the lead or to have something to exploit. Well, I've got both."

"Who is it?"

"John Wayne."

John Wayne?" Jimmy didn't understand. "You're gonna have to explain this to me, because first of all, John Wayne's deader than disco. In fact, I think they both died at about the same time. Second, I'm pretty sure John Wayne was making more to appear in a picture back in the Seventies than your entire movie's got for a budget."

Edison laughed, pointing to his temple. "I've got all the bases covered."

Jimmy just stared at him, cutting off a corner of pepperoni and anchovy pizza with his fork.

"My girlfriend, Bree, practices witchcraft," Edison said. "She's got a spell book that's supposed to raise the dead and make them do your bidding. Well, we're gonna use that spell to raise John Wayne and make him appear in our movie."

"You're crazy," said Jimmy.

"Like a fox."

"Okay, so why John Wayne?"

"Why *not* John Wayne?" Edison asked. "He's my favorite actor. I'd love to be able to say I directed him in a movie. The man's a friggin' icon."

"Will he be able to speak? I mean, he's been dead for almost forty years."

"We're not sure yet."

"Your girlfriend has never used this spell before?"

"No," Edison said. "That kind of thing doesn't come up every day."

"He probably looks pretty rough these days."

"Which will be just fine since it's a zombie movie. So whaddaya think?"

"Well," Jimmy said, "It would look good on my resume to have made a movie with John Wayne."

Edison nodded. "Now you're talking."

At that point the waitress came over and asked if they needed anything.

"I'll have orange juice," Edison said.

"I'm sorry, but we don't have orange juice."

Edison grinned. "Why don't you go in the back and see if you can find some. After all, I'm a famous movie director, and you're gonna want my return business."

The woman grimaced and stalked off towards the kitchen.

"That was kind of a dick thing to do," Jimmy said.

"Hey," Edison said, "all the big directors do it. So are you on board?"

"It looks like I am. But I'd like to talk about my financial package."

"How so?"

"I'm gonna need three hundred dollars to make the movie."

Edison raised his hand and they shook on it.

Two weeks later, Edison, his buddy and producer Parker, and his girlfriend, Bree, were standing over John Wayne's grave at the Pacific View Memorial Park Cemetery in Corona del Mar. There was a full moon out, which Bree said was a must for such an occasion. It was dark outside otherwise, and there was a cool breeze blowing. Bree had used sidewalk chalk to draw a humongous pink pentagram over the grave, as well as some words in a dead language around the grave.

"You think this'll work?" asked Parker.

"I do," said Bree. "I've used several other spells from this book and they all work."

Bree opened the book and started reading from the dead language of Akkadian. "Cheepa, cheepa, burga, cheep," she said. Edison and Parker repeated the words, and Bree continued. Finally, after about ten minutes of this, the wind picked up and it started to rain.

"What the fuck?" asked Edison.

"We're upsetting the gods," said Bree.

"Does that mean it's working?"

"Yeah," she said. "I think so."

She read more Akkadian. "Beygo, teehum, daydo, bohah..."

After several minutes of this, she closed the book and stood silently. Suddenly the rain stopped.

"What is it?" asked Parker.

"The spell is complete," she said.

"But I don't see John Wayne," said Edison.

Bree pointed down at the grave. "He's reanimated, but he's down there, in his coffin, unable to get out."

"So now what?" asked Parker.

Edison shrugged. "We go to the car and get the shovels and we dig."

And they did just that. Edison and Parker dug for two hours. Bree sat on a nearby grave and painted her fingernails and toes.

Chunk! came the sound from inside the grave.

"Hey, I've hit the coffin," Edison said. "We're almost there."

Once they had the coffin fully excavated, they found great difficulty in getting it open inside the hole they had dug. But finally they managed to do just that. When Edison opened the coffin, a wickedly rotten stench emerged. With the moon behind the clouds and the flashlight lying on the ground, they could barely see inside the box.

And then, suddenly, the reanimated corpse lunged out of its coffin and seized Parker, chewing on his face.

"Arrrggggghhhh!" screamed Parker.

The corpse was gnawing off Parker's nose.

Edison backed away, watching his friend being eaten.

"Should we help him?" asked Bree.

"By 'we' you mean 'me,'" said Edison, still watching the gruesome sight.

The reanimated corpse of John Wayne was grotesque, like something out of an Italian horror movie. He was missing an ear, his skull was exposed under rotten, leathery flesh, he smelled terrible, and there were tiny maggots falling out of his ear holes and empty eye sockets. And now what was left of his face was covered in Parker's fresh blood.

"What do I do?" asked Edison nervously.

"You command him to stop eating Parker."

"John Wayne," Edison said. "Stop eating that man—*now*!"

And the reanimated corpse of John Wayne stopped feasting on Edison's dead friend and producer. Through the power of command, Edison was able to subdue the corpse while he filled in the grave over Parker's half-eaten body. Although Bree wasn't fond of having maggots falling all over the back seat of her Honda Civic, the three of them drove back to Edison's house in silence.

They were two days into shooting, and Edison and his two-man crew were filming on a hand-held digital camera inside an apartment in Silver Lake. The reanimated corpse of John Wayne was hitting his marks. Of course he couldn't talk, but Edison filmed him staggering around and waving his arms just the same.

"Unnnngggghhhh!" growled John Wayne.

It was a scene between John Wayne and Sarah Newsom, one of Edison's regulars. Sarah was topless and in the middle of a lengthy monologue when John Wayne reached out and grabbed her head at both sides, twisting it hard. Her neck made a sickening crunching sound as he did this.

"Dammit, John Wayne!" Edison said.

But John Wayne didn't give a damn. He was leaned forward and was chewing into the dead actress's skull.

"John Wayne, stop that!" Edison said. John Wayne just looked up with a mouth full of brains, chewing. The bottom part of his jaw fell off as he did this, and a bunch of maggots fell out of his mouth into Sarah's skull.

"Phil," Edison said. "Can you please find a way to reattach John Wayne's lower jaw?"

Phil, the film's P.A., nervously walked towards John Wayne, still trying to feast on the dead Sarah with his bottom jaw missing. Phil turned his head, sizing up the damage. "I think I can reattach it with some putty," Phil said. But just then, John Wayne reached out and grabbed Phil's hand, pulling it to his face. He attempted to chew off Phil's fingers, but got nowhere without his bottom jaw. Phil tried to pull his maggot-covered hand away, but John Wayne dropped Sarah's body and grabbed Phil's arm with both of his own, tearing it out of the socket.

Phil screamed in agony.

"Goddammit, John Wayne!" Edison said, turning to his crew. "This is why I don't like using 'name' talent. They're all prima donnas. If they're not rewriting the dialogue on set, they're eating the cast and crew!"

Edison sat down the camera and turned to go and grab a tuna fish sandwich from the craft service table. He exhaled heavily as he walked, now fully irritated. He heard more screams behind him, but he didn't turn around. He was now second-guessing his decision to reanimate John Wayne. This was gonna be one hell of a long shoot. They were only two days in and already way behind schedule.

DOBIE'S LAST RIDE

Cam Nicholson really, really hated Dobie, his children's big Black Labrador. He fucking loathed him. And he couldn't say for sure, for who knew what went on inside the mind of a dog, but he was pretty sure Dobie felt the same way about him. Cam's two kids, Jeffrey, age eight, and Leia, age seven, had adopted the old dog the previous summer with permission from their mother, the household softy. Things had been okay throughout the summer, although Cam didn't really care for the dog even then, but had grown considerably worse once the children had gone back to school, leaving him alone with the dog each day.

Cam was a stay-at-home novelist. One day he had left a working manuscript of his third novel, *The Toxicity of Snakes*, lying on the floor beside his desk. Dobie being Dobie, he urinated all over it, causing the ink to run wildly across the pages. Cam had tried his best to laugh the whole thing off, calling Dobie the world's toughest critic, but he was still pretty irritated about the whole thing. Dobie rarely pissed on anything, but if Cam left something out, it got pissed on. Dobie rarely chewed on anything, but if Cam left something important lying out, it got chewed all to hell.

What we have here, folks, is a showdown, Cam thought. *A battle of wills.*

One afternoon Cam was masturbating and watching porn on his computer—just some regular old vanilla guy-on-girl stuff—when he noticed Dobie sitting beside the desk, watching him intently with what appeared to be a judgmental expression.

"Fuck you, Dobie," Cam said, tossing the bottle of lotion at him with his free hand.

But Dobie just sat there, looking stupid, continuing to stare.

Cam stood up, his pants around his ankles, and grabbed the stupid dog by the scruff of his neck. He then began dragging him out of the room, mad at himself for not shutting the door in the first place, when Dobie got free and bit his hand.

"Ouch!" Cam screamed, investigating the bite, which was already bleeding. He looked down at Dobie with his pants still around his ankles, and began to curse the damned animal, calling him everything but a good dog. He pulled up his pants and escorted Dobie out of the room, kicking him as he did so. Cam then went back to finish the deed, but found that he could not continue masturbating as his hand was now bloodied and hurt like hell. He glared at the door, as if the animal could see him through it, and as if he'd understand the glare even if he could.

Things had been rough for Cam lately, and although it wasn't Dobie's fault, he found himself now allowing all of his disappointment and anger to fall down squarely upon the dumb animal's haunches.

First of all, *The Toxicity of Snakes* was due in less than two weeks, and Cam was nowhere close to being finished with it. He'd gotten halfway through the thing before realizing he'd taken an unneeded detour that had taken him a good hundred pages out of his way. Now all that work had to be scrapped and he faced the daunting task of having to basically start over at the beginning of act two. He'd tried to explain this to his agent, Mitch, but it was to no avail. Mitch just kept on insisting that he finish the book in record time. It was so easy for someone who didn't write to tell him how to go about writing his novel. Now Mitch was saying Hill House Publishing might opt out of the entire deal if the manuscript wasn't ready on time.

Then, making matters worse, Cam and his wife had been fighting lately. He knew it was because of the pressures brought about by the novel, but that knowledge did little to stop the arguments. One night the two of them had been arguing when their little girl, Leia, came into the room and screamed, "Daddy, stop yelling at Mommy!" As if the whole thing was his fault. Even though he knew deep down that a great deal of it was in fact his fault, he still felt that his wife should share at least some of the blame. So now his kids looked at him like he was a monster. He did his best to please them, taking them to the movies to see the blockbuster superhero movie of the month, even buying them Cokes and popcorn, but they still thought he was an ass.

The day after the masturbation/biting incident, Cam discovered that Dobie had chewed through the electrical cord to his printer. He then looked at Dobie, swearing the damned animal was grinning at him.

And Cam realized for the first time that he really hated that dog with every fiber of his being. That damned dog was the bane of his existence, a four-legged arch-enemy.

Fuck it, he thought. It was time for old Dobie to go on a one-way car trip to Doggie Land. Sure, his kids would be upset, but fuck them, too, for treating him like an asshole. Dropping Dobie off in the country would be poetic justice for everyone involved.

Cam picked up Dobie, hoisting him over his shoulder. The dog did not growl, didn't act one way or the other about the whole thing. He just let Cam carry him out to the car. Cam fumbled with the door handle, Dobie still in his arms, and barely got the thing open. He placed Dobie inside the car on the passenger's seat.

"Sit tight, little buddy," he said, going around the car and climbing into the driver's side. He put the key into the ignition, starting the car, the sounds of liberal talk radio filling the tiny Prius. Cam backed the car out of the driveway into the gravel road which ran parallel with the house, and started driving east. He drove for several miles, looking around as carefully as a man in the country searching for a spot to take a leak, and finally stopped the car.

Cam got out, still looking around to make sure he wasn't being watched, and made his way around the Prius. He opened the door, called for Dobie to get his black ass out, and then shut the door behind him. As he walked back around to the driver's side, watching Dobie just sitting there like the big dumb animal he was, Cam waved. "Ta-ta, Dobie!" He climbed back into the car, turned it around in an entrance to a wheat field, and headed towards home. He looked back in the rearview mirror, watching Dobie just sitting there, growing smaller and smaller in the distance.

Good riddance to bad dogs, he thought, turning up the radio to hear an interview with Al Gore about the current state of global warming. "Only an idiot would not believe in global warming at this point," Gore was saying. Cam laughed, thinking, *stupid fucking Dobie probably didn't believe in global warming*. This led to another thought—that now Dobie could actually experience those weather changes from outside in the weather himself— and Cam chuckled again.

As he approached his home, he knew he would just barely make it before the kids' bus dropped them off from school. When he came over the hill where his house was, he saw that the bus wasn't there yet and breathed a sigh of relief. As he pulled the little silver Prius into the driveway, he saw something peculiar—Dobie was sitting on the porch, waiting for him, looking as though nothing out of the ordinary had happened.

What the fuck? Cam thought. *How can this be possible?*

There was no way Dobie ran all that way home, faster than Cam's car. It just wasn't possible, and Cam would have seen him past by if he had. *And look at him*, Cam thought—the damned dog didn't look tired in the least. He looked completely normal and unshaken.

Cam got out of the car and moved slowly towards the dog. As he did so, the school bus came over the hill, approaching the house. Cam walked over and petted Dobie's head. He knew it was madness on his part, but he swore he saw a smug glint in the deep blackness of the dog's eyes. "You and I are gonna have to bury the hatchet and pretend everything's okay for the kiddos," Cam said quietly, still petting the dog's head. "But tomorrow's another story. Tomorrow you and I are gonna go round-and-round, partner. I promise you that, Dobie old boy."

The bus stopped and its doors hissed open. Jeffrey and Leia came rushing up to the porch, climbing all over Dobie. "Dobie!" Leia squealed. "He's my best friend." Jeffrey rubbed the dog's turned head, and Dobie seemed to be staring at Cam again. "You'll never beat me," his eyes seemed to say. "For I am Dobie the Great, you stupid, insignificant motherfucker."

Cam just shook it off and went back inside the house.

The next day Cam fed Dobie a can of chicken Alpo with a bit of rat poison on top for lunch. Cam felt like shit about the whole deal, but he didn't want to see this dog turn up again. It was too much damned work driving him all over the country as if he were being chauffeured. Shortly after eating the meal, Dobie started to act drowsy and lay down on the carpet.

"That's it, Dobie, old boy," Cam said. "Just go to sleep. Nighty-night."

Cam lifted the dog in his arms once again, this time feeling more like Dobie was dead weight than he had been before. He carried the canine out to the car, opened the door, and sat him inside the passenger's side, where he just laid down on the seat, looking drowsy as hell.

Cam climbed into the Prius again, switched talk radio over to John Denver singing "Thank God I'm a Country Boy" on some AM soft-rock oldies station. Cam pulled out of the drive again, tapping his fingers on the steering wheel to the rhythm of the song.

He looked over at Dobie. "I'm sorry, old boy, but I really have to get rid of you. I can't have you fucking up my shit anymore. And my kids love you...if they knew what was happening here, they'd never forgive me. Hell, they probably love you more than they love me. But that won't be a problem—not anymore."

This time Cam drove a full six miles, finally finding an open clearing in the middle of nowhere. He got out of the car, walked briskly around to Dobie's side, opened the door, and called for the dog. Dobie didn't move. He was still awake, still alive, barely, but wasn't doing much moving. Cam hefted the old dog out of the seat, laid him on the gravel, where Dobie promptly tried to go back to sleep. Cam walked around and climbed back into the Prius. As he drove away, he watched Dobie lying there, looking dead already, buried in a cloud of kicked-up gravel dust. Again, he felt terrible that things had to be this way, but it if it was either Dobie or him, he was damned sure he was going to be the victor.

When Cam came rolling over the hill to his house, he was much happier, singing along to Elton John's "Rocket Man." He pulled into the drive and stopped the car.

And his heart almost stopped.

There, on the porch, was Dobie, sitting upright, looking as healthy as ever, staring at him with his dark black eyes.

Motherfucker! Cam thought. *Motherfucking motherfucker!*

And as Cam pulled himself out of the Prius, he heard the sounds of the bus pulling up behind him. The kids were home.

Cam just stared at the dog, wishing him death.

The children climbed off the bus and ran past him, rushing up to Dobie, smothering him with their love. And as they did, Dobie just stared at Cam, a cold look in his eyes. Cam knew it was impossible—after all, Dobie was just a stupid animal—but he also knew what he saw.

That night Cam didn't sleep well. He kept the door shut against his wife Camille's wishes, secretly afraid of Dobie attacking him in his sleep. And when he finally managed to go to sleep, he had a string of dreams about Dobie.

The next morning Cam was ready for the little bastard. He started his doggie battles early on this particular day, planning to be well-finished before the kids got out of school. No sooner than the kids' bus had left and Camille was off on her way to work, Cam went to his bedroom closet. There he reached up, feeling around on a high shelf, and removed the Colt .45 his grandfather had given him from World War II. He went to a drawer in the kitchen, removed a handful of bullets, and loaded the pistol, feeling powerful with the gun in his hand.

When he turned around, that feeling subsided; he was startled to see the big black dog sitting there, staring at him coldly. "Come on, motherfucker, I dare you," Dobie seemed to say. "I double-dog dare you."

Game on, Cam thought. He tucked the old .45 into his waistline, lifted Dobie up into his arms, and took him out to the Prius once again. He opened the car door, pushed the dog inside on the passenger's side, and walked back to the garage to get a shovel. He then climbed into the driver's side and switched on the car. "Summer Breeze" by Seals and Croft came floating out from the radio. *No, not today*, thought Cam. Today was an AC/DC day all the way. He opened the glove compartment as Dobie watched, and grabbed the CD. He slid it into the CD player, pushed the buttons, and "Dirty Deeds Done Dirt Cheap" came blasting out from the speakers.

Cam looked at Dobie. "You ready to take your last ride, motherfucker?"

But Dobie did not answer.

Cam backed out of the driveway and drove the Prius east. This time he went a full ten miles out into the middle of nowhere before stopping the car. He looked around again, making sure no one was around, and went to the passenger side of the car. He opened the door, pulled Dobie out by the back of his neck, and drug him into the road.

Cam slid the .45 out of his waistline, staring down at the dog.

Dobie said nothing, but his eyes seemed to laugh at him.

What the fuck? Cam thought. *Stupid dog.*

"I wouldn't be so smug if I were you, asshole," Cam said, raising the pistol, training it on the dog's face. He squeezed the trigger. *Blam! Blam! Blam!*

And Dobie was dead, lying there in a bloodied heap.

Cam then carried him into the woods just beyond the tree line, and dug a shallow grave, laying the dog inside once he was finished. He then shoveled dirt back over the hole, burying the dead animal. Not wanting to be caught doing this particular bit of villainy, Cam ran back to the Prius, stuck the shovel inside, climbed in, turned the car around, and sped away.

He knew it was impossible, knew it couldn't possibly happen, but still found himself wondering if Dobie would be sitting there on the porch when he got home, looking like the smug little cocksucker he was. Cam sped like a madman all the way home, rocking out to AC/DC's "Back in Black."

And when Cam came flying over the hill to his house, he looked up at the porch—and there was no Dobie there!

"Holy shit!" Cam screamed. "Praise be unto big fat baby Jesus! Ding-dong, Dobie's dead!" Cam looked into the mirror and spoke to his own reflection. "You did it, old man. You killed the beast. *You killed the fucking beast!*"

Cam chuckled, regained his composure, and stuck the .45 in the glove compartment. He walked quickly into the house, feeling an extra spring in his step. He also felt a little something in his stomach... He went immediately to the restroom, slid down his pants, and sat on the toilet, humming happily as he did his business. Damn, what putting a bullet into an asshole Black Lab did for a man's mood. He reached down into the magazine rack beside the toilet, fished out an aged issue of *Entertainment Weekly*, and flipped it open to a story about Beyonce.

And then he heard it.

It was quiet at first but got louder as it continued.

Growling.

It was Dobie, now inside the bathroom, moving towards him, growling an evil growl. Dobie was filthy, still wearing the soil from his grave on his fur. Cam was scared to death. If he hadn't already been taking a shit, he would have shit himself right there. He was frozen, his muscles all locked up, sitting there on the commode as Dobie moved toward him. And as Dobie moved ever closer, he continued to growl, strings of slobber hanging from his mouth as he did.

And he lunged.

The school bus pulled up in front of the house at three-thirty. The doors hissed open, and Jeffrey and Leia climbed off the bus. They ran up to the porch, where Dobie was sitting there waiting for them. They found Dobie to be as happy as ever, but noticed dried blood and dirt in his hair.

"Is he hurt?" Leia asked.

"I don't think so," Jeffrey said, feeling around on the dog's head.

There was, however, one thing out of the ordinary. Normally their father waited for them on the porch alongside Dobie, but today he was nowhere to be seen.

"Where's Dad?" Leia asked.

"Who cares?" answered Jeffrey.

They rubbed all over Dobie's fur, and he almost looked as though he was smiling with joy. He loved his children, and his children loved him, too, and nothing would ever come between them now.

THE HOLLISTER JOB

Redd had only been out of the joint for a week, and here he was scoping out a new bank to rob. The bank, the swankiest he'd ever seen, promised a big payday if everything went right. The First Hollister Bank was set right in the middle of posh Beverly Hills, and had as many flashy accoutrements as a Catholic church.

Redd had never seen anything like this. The Hollister had four or five big, bronze statues of various Forefathers, copious Baroque-style paintings featuring all kinds of Americana, huge, gaudy chandeliers dangling overhead, and expensive marble floors to boot. This place was nicer than The White House. Redd was here to set up a bank account, sizing up the place as he did.

Oh yes, there was big money here all right. Big money.

And soon, if everything went as planned, at least part of it would be his.

But he knew there was a lot that could go wrong. His crew was way less professional than those he was used to working with back in New York. They were basically chain-snatchers and coke-heads, but he figured they'd be all right for one friggin' job. One huge score, the payday to end all paydays—the one on which Redd could finally retire from the life.

After setting up his bank account, the generically-pretty blond told him, "Please come back and see us again soon."

"Oh, I will," he said, smiling at her.

He could tell she was feeling him, wanting to have sex with him, and he thought he might just come back and take her out to dinner once this job was behind him. But for now there was no time for such thoughts. Now was the most important part of any heist—the planning period, in which all of the little details were worked out in advance so there would be no fuck ups when the day came.

Eight days later, Redd was back at The Hollister. Beansy pulled the Buick up to the front of the place at a quarter to three, and Redd and his crew climbed out and approached the doors. Each of them was wearing a long raincoat, their shotguns hidden by their sides. They pulled the pantyhose over their heads, concealing their faces. Once he was through the door, Redd brought the shotgun up, pointing it at the old, fat security guard standing there. The other three men piled into the door behind him.

Redd pointed at the doors. "Lock them now or you die," he told the security guard.

The frightened old man did as he was told

Redd, Darryl, Mook, and Carl quickly spread out so they could cover everyone inside the bank. Their shotguns were up, and they were ready for whatever might come their way. There was a smattering of people inside the bank—mostly women and a couple of kids.

"Everyone lay down on the fucking floor!" Redd screamed. "Don't make me say it twice. Anyone tries to play Bruce Willis hero, you die, and then the person next to you dies just because you were such an asshole!"

Redd rushed to the front counter, climbing on top of it, waving his shotgun wildly. As he figured it, they had about three minutes to get the money and get the fuck out. Redd lowered the barrel of the shotgun at the clerk, still standing, and told her to gather up his money.

"Anybody hits the silent alarm, they die," he said matter-of-factly. "If I don't know who did it, you all die. Simple as that."

Redd jumped down behind the counter, rushing towards a meek, middle-aged man wearing a tie.

"You the manager?" he asked.

The frightened man said nothing.

Redd raised the shotgun up under his chin.

"I'll repeat myself only once," he said. "Are. You. The. Manager?"

"Yes," the man said, about to piss himself.

"You open up that fucking vault now, or everyone here dies."

"I can't."

"What?"

"I can't open it. It's locked for the rest of the day."

"You're the fucking manager. You can open that door."

"I can't."

Redd turned slightly to his right and shot one of the clerks lying on the ground. The blast blew her back wide open, blood now covering her white blouse, and her now-dead body slid several inches on the marble floor.

24

He turned back to the manager.

"Tell me you can't open that door again."

"I-I-I can't," the man said.

Redd turned to his left and shot another clerk down on the floor. The shotgun blast struck the man's head, leaving a two-foot streak of blood and brains splattered across the floor.

Now he had the shotgun raised back to the manager's face.

"What's your name?" Redd asked.

"Mark."

"Mark, you open that door or so help me god I'll kill every motherfucker in here, including those kids."

Mark looked over at the kids.

"You do see the kids out there, don't you, Mark?"

"Yes."

"Then open that vault."

"You could kill everyone in here, and I still wouldn't be able to open it."

Redd was getting pissed.

He looked at Carl. "You take one of the kids—the little boy—into the back and you shoot him in the goddamn head."

"Why in the back?" asked Carl.

"Because he's a little fucking kid," Redd said. "It would be distasteful to kill him out here."

Carl snatched up the kid, dragging him. The kid's wailing mother tried to protest, but Carl kicked her in the face, rendering her unconscious. As Carl dragged the boy around the counter, Redd turned back to Mark.

"So help me god, Mark, I'll do it."

"I believe you."

"But you still won't open the vault?"

"I can't."

"How much money you make here?"

"What?"

"That's not your money back there. You're a fucking lackey. Is that money worth dying for, Mark?"

"I-I-I..."

"Now please open the vault, Mark. Pretty please, sugar on top."

"I can't."

And that's when Redd shot the manager.

Carl was dragging the kid towards a back room of the bank. The kid was crying, kicking up a fuss, and fighting him. Then the kid bit him on the hand.

"*Fuck!*" screamed Carl, backhanding the boy.

They were now in a hallway, out of sight from the rest of the bank's patrons, and Carl decided to just get it over with right here and now. He raised the shotgun at the little bastard, whose eyes got big. The little boy started to back up, sobbing hard now.

Carl's finger was on the trigger, and he was starting to squeeze it.

Then he saw the boy looking up at something behind him.

He turned and saw the figure looming over him.

"What the fuck?" he asked.

It was the six-foot-tall bronze statue of George Washington. The statue reached out and grabbed Carl's head, lifting it up. It raised Carl off the ground, his feet kicking beneath him. George Washington twisted the head with a gruesome crunch, tearing it from its body. The statue looked down at the little boy, now stunned into silence, and tossed Carl's head onto the ground at his feet.

The little boy let out a loud scream, piercing the momentary silence.

Out front, Redd was wondering what all the fuss was.

Why hadn't he heard the shotgun blast yet?

He could hear police sirens approaching, and he was starting to freak out. He did not want to go back to prison. Redd was about to go and check on Carl and the little boy, but was stopped in his tracks when he heard the police bullhorn outside the bank.

"We know you're in there," the cop said. "Release the hostages and come out with your hands up. It's not too late. Everyone can live through this."

And Beansy fired a shotgun blast through the glass window at the cops.

"Dammit, Beansy!" screamed Redd.

This was getting out of hand.

Redd could see now there were cops all around the building.

"Get the fuck out of here, pigs!" he screamed, knowing it was to no avail. Hell, they probably couldn't even hear him at this distance.

Then the telephone rang. Redd knew it was the cops, knew it was for him. He looked at the single standing clerk, a woman, who asked, "You gonna answer that?"

He picked up the phone, looking out the window. "Yeah?"

"We've got you surrounded," the pig said. "We need you to let the hostages go if you're gonna make it out of this alive. And we need you to stop shooting. No shooting at us, and no shooting at the hostages."

Redd thought about it.

"I want a million dollars cash," Redd said. "I want a million dollars, and I want a helicopter to come and get us and take us away from here."

"You really think that's gonna work?" asked the cop.

"It could work."

"When has that plan *ever* worked?"

Redd got angry and threw the telephone receiver. He looked at Mook. "Shoot the other kid," he told him. Mook moved forward towards the little girl and pulled her up by her hair.

"Stand up," he told her flatly.

Redd knew what he was seeing, but he couldn't believe it.

As Mook stood over the girl, about to shoot her, a figure approached him from behind. It was the big, bronze statue of Benjamin Franklin, holding his bronze kite. The statue reached out its arm, kite in hand, and brought the thing swooping down to slice off Mook's head with its sharp edge. The bank robber's head sat in place atop his neck for a moment, and then his eyes rolled up into its head, and then the head toppled to the ground, bouncing on the marble floor.

"*What the fuck?*" screamed Redd.

Redd could see that Darryl's eyes were as big as saucers, even with the pantyhose over his face. Darryl looked at him. "You ain't paying me enough for this shit! I'm getting out of here!"

Darryl turned to run, but bronze John Adams was there to block his path. The statue grabbed him and pulled, ripping both of his arms out of their sockets. The shotgun went off when it struck the floor, but no one jumped. Everyone in the lobby of the bank just stood or lay with their eyes glued to that big, bronze statue.

Redd turned back towards the hallway where Carl had taken the boy. He now saw the crying boy emerge, blood covering his face, but there was no Carl to be seen. Redd rushed towards the boy, snatching him up. He raised the shotgun to the side of the crying boy's head.

They weren't going to take him alive.

Redd wasn't going back to prison.

"*I've got a kid!*" Redd screamed towards the lights outside the broken window. "*I swear I'll kill him if you don't let me out of here!*"

But Redd failed to see the Thomas Jefferson statue emerging from the shadows. The boy's eyes got big looking at the statue. Redd saw his reaction and knew something was behind him, but he couldn't turn in time. He dropped the boy and his shotgun when he felt Thomas Jefferson's fist being rammed up his ass.

Redd screamed a piercing scream, but no one came to help.

Police Chief Hal Siegelman was standing there inside the bank where the robbery had taken place, staring at the statue. "Damnedest thing I ever heard," he said.

Corporal Tillman asked, "You believe any of it?"

Siegelman wanted to laugh, but couldn't. "Mass hysteria. There's no other way to explain what these people say they saw."

"But how do you think the statue got way back here behind the counter? And how did the other statues end up moved all over the bank?"

"I dunno," said Siegelman, his eyes still glued to the statue.

"More importantly, how do you think the robber got up there?"

Siegelman said nothing. He just stared at the bronze statue with its bloody arm raised to the sky, its bronze fist still stuck up the dangling bank robber's ass.

THE DEAD MAN'S LULLABY

The young man from the pharmacy delivered Betty's medications early in the afternoon. Betty liked him very much. He reminded her of her nephew, Darryl, whom she rarely saw these days. It was a warm May day, and Betty sat out on the front porch talking with the young man for several minutes. She didn't know how old he was, as age was something that had become extremely difficult for her to gauge in her later years. But she figured he was probably in his twenties, as he was old enough to drive and old enough to have respect for his elders. The two of them talked about the weather mostly, and then Betty gave him a quarter tip before he left.

After sitting on the porch, enjoying the warmth of the day for another few minutes, Betty finally went back into the drab, dreary old house. She took her medications into her bedroom, setting them and her pill counter out on the bed so she could divide them up for the coming week. As she did, she glanced at the old dusty radio sitting on the dresser. She hadn't played it in years, but now thought a little soft music might be nice as she prepared her meds. She switched on the radio, a loud buzz drowning out the tinny, distant sound of music. She turned the knob, searching for something soft that would come in a little clearer. There was mostly just static on the old radio, and she briefly wondered if it would work at all. As she was turning, she heard a frail voice emerge from within the static.

"Betty," the voice said.

It took her a moment to register what she'd heard, and by the time she did, she'd already passed the station where she'd heard it. She knew it wasn't possible that the radio was speaking directly to her, but she turned the knob back slowly, finally settling on the channel once again.

It was faint, but it was there.

"Betty."

The voice was familiar, but she couldn't immediately identify it.

"Betty," the voice said again. "Betty, my dear, is that you?"

Now Betty recognized it.

It was her dead husband, Bill. It couldn't possibly be, but she knew it was.

"Betty, my dear..."

"Yes?" she managed.

"That is you, isn't it?" the voice said.

She gulped. "Yes, it's me."

"It's Bill."

"I know who you are," said Betty. "We were married for sixty-one years."

"I love you, Betty."

She felt herself tearing up. "I love you, too, Bill."

"How are you? How have you been, my dear?"

"Alone," she said. "I've been alone."

"I'm sorry, Betty," he said, sadness filling his frail voice.

"I've missed you these last few years."

"I've missed you, too."

"Can I ask you a question?" asked Betty.

"Anything, my dear."

"Where are you?"

Bill laughed happily. "I guess this is heaven. I don't know for sure. Nobody tells you. But it's beautiful here; bright, stunning colors like a Van Gogh painting. It's so relaxed. And best of all, there's no pain."

"You're not in pain anymore?"

"Oh, no," said Bill. "I feel wonderful."

"But you're dead."

"I am, aren't I?" He chuckled again.

"Can you see me?" Betty asked. "Do you watch over me?"

"No, dear, I can't see you."

"How are we speaking now? How does this work?"

"I don't know," said Bill. "They don't tell you anything here."

"Are there others there?"

"Oh, yes, lots of others."

"Are they happy, too?"

"Everyone is happy here."

"Are there people there that you know—from *before*?"

"Oh, yes."

"Like who? Who's there?"

"Michael's here, Betty."

Betty's mind turned to her dead son, drowned at the age of ten, and she started to cry.

"He...is?" she asked, her voice cracking.

"Yes, Betty. He's here and he's wonderful."

"Is he still ten?"

"No," Bill said. "Everyone here is an adult. You should see the man he's become."

"Really?"

"My brother Sam is here, and..."

"My sister, Theresa?"

"She's here, too, Betty. We're all just waiting for you."

"You are?"

She felt her heart soar just a bit.

"We think about you all the time."

"You do?"

"Of course," said Bill. "You're my baby girl."

Betty was choked up, couldn't speak.

"You okay, Betty, my dear?"

"It's just a lot for me to take in," she said.

Bill said, "I'm sure it is. Give it some time, old girl. Give it time."

"It's so good to hear your voice."

"It's terrific hearing your voice, too."

"I miss you so much."

"I miss you, too."

There was a long silence, and Betty tried to regain her composure. She tried to look at this objectively. Was she losing her mind? She was talking to her long-dead husband through an AM radio. It just wasn't possible.

But it was.

"Betty?"

"Yes, Bill?"

"I've got to go."

"But you just got here. I've waited so long to talk to you."

"It's gonna be okay, Betty."

"Will you be back?"

"Oh, yes," Bill said. "Now that I've got you again, I'll never let you go."

Betty said, "I love you, Bill." Saying the words felt so familiar on her tongue.

"I love you, too."

"Goodbye."

"Until next time, my love."

And Bill was gone, leaving only static behind.

Betty didn't know how to process all this. She felt she had to be losing her mind. Every minute that passed without her hearing Bill's voice she became more and more certain she was having a nervous breakdown.

She knelt down next to her bed and she prayed to God for answers.

Finally she arose and went to the phone. She dialed it, the radio static still crackling behind her.

"Hello?" answered Terry, her minister.

"Terry?"

"Yes?"

"Terry, this is Betty Buckley. I have a problem."

"Okay, I'll help in any way I can, Sister Betty."

"Thank you in advance."

"What seems to be the problem?"

Betty said, "It's Bill."

"Bill?" Terry asked, weighing the name. "Your *husband*, Bill?"

"One and the same."

"What about him, Betty?"

"He's talking to me."

There was a long pause on the other end of the phone and then Terry said, "Our loved ones speak to us in a variety of ways from beyond the gates of heaven. How exactly is Bill speaking to you, Betty?"

"I know how this is gonna sound," Betty said. "But I'm hearing his voice."

"His voice?"

"On my radio."

"Uh," said Terry. "How so?"

"He speaks to me."

"What does he say?"

"He tells me he loves me," said Betty. "And that he's in heaven with our son, Michael. And my sister. And his brother..."

Silence again. "I'll tell you what: how about I come over there and listen to the radio with you? Do you think he'll talk to me?"

"I don't see why not," Betty said. "But he's not there all the time."

"How many times have you heard him?"

"Only once so far."

"How do you know he'll be back?"

Betty said, "Because he told me so.."

Betty waited thirty-five minutes for Terry to arrive at her house. She led him into her dreary old bedroom and asked him to sit on the bed. She walked over and switched on the radio, hunkering down over it.

All they heard was static.

Terry looked at her, trying to conceal the expression which said she was pathetic.

"Maybe if we wait for a few minutes he'll show up," said Betty.

"That sounds like a good idea."

"I wonder if it's the right station."

"What do you mean?"

"He didn't say if he would always be on the same station. I mean, he was on that one then, but who knows about next time?"

Terry looked concerned. "So they have a radio station in heaven?"

"I don't think so. I mean, I don't know."

"What do you think happened?"

"I don't think he was at a radio station or anything. I think he was just talking to me from heaven, and it was coming out of my radio."

"Could he hear you?" asked Terry. "Did you try to talk back?"

"Oh, yes, we had quite a conversation."

"What did he say?"

"Just that he missed me. And he said that he loved me."

"Of course."

"And like I said, he told me Michael was there, too."

"Right."

"He said heaven was bright with pretty colors, like a Vincent Van Gogh painting."

"Van Gogh, huh?"

"And he said there's no pain where he's at."

"Why, that does sound nice," he said, clearly humoring her.

"I promise you Bill was here, on this radio."

"I believe you."

She made a face. "You do?"

He said he did, but she saw through it.

"Do you still think he's gonna come and talk to me?" asked Terry.

"I don't know. I promise you, he was here."

"I believe you."

"He said he loved me."

She started to sob again.

Terry put his arm around her shoulder. "Why don't you and I pray about this?"

They prayed, the sound of radio static still filling the room. Terry's prayer sounded simultaneously concerned and condescending, but Betty thought maybe she was reading too much into it. When Terry was finished with the prayer, he looked at her, holding her frail hands in his own.

"What do you think happened here?" she asked.

"The Lord works in mysterious ways."

"Do you honestly believe Bill was here, talking through my radio?"

"I don't know what exactly I believe," said Terry. "But I do believe that you believe it, and that's enough for me. It sounds like it was a very sweet conversation. Real or imagined, do you know what most people would give to have one last conversation with their dearly departed?"

Betty frowned. She hoped it wouldn't be her last conversation with Bill.

Later that evening, as Betty was watching *Wheel of Fortune*, the phone rang. She answered it, and it was her daughter, Kelly.

"Mom?"

"Yes, dear?"

"I, uh, talked with your minister."

Betty didn't like that one bit. She had trusted Terry, and he had betrayed that trust.

"He called you, did he?" asked Betty.

"He's worried about you."

Betty said nothing.

"I'm worried about you, Mom."

"There's no need for anyone to worry about me."

"He said you're talking to Dad. On an AM radio."

"This is none of your business, Kelly. If I had wanted to share this with you, I would have called you myself."

"This isn't normal, Mom."

Betty questioned her sanity again. Was she losing her mind? Was everyone else correct? She didn't know the answer, but she wasn't about to just give in and let them lock her away in some damned old folks home.

"I'm telling you, I'm fine," said Betty.

"I don't know what to think about this."

"What does Terry think?"

"He's worried."

"He thinks I'm crazy, doesn't he?"

"He's just worried about you," Kelly said. "We're all worried about you."

"No need to worry about me. You need to worry about yourself."

Kelly sighed. "What does that mean?"

"You and Ted split up every six months. That's what it means. Maybe you need to worry more about your own problems and less about mine."

"That's not fair, Mom."

"Then don't you call me trying to determine if I'm crazy," said Betty. "I'm still the mother here, not you. You don't get to question me."

"But, Mom."

"What?"

"Dad's dead."

"Don't you think I know that?" Betty asked. "I'm the one who has to live here day in and day out alone without him. I'm fully aware that your father is dead."

"But Terry said you're talking to him."

"And he talks to me," said Betty. "So what? What business is it of yours?"

"Dead people don't talk, Mom. They don't. Dad can't talk to anyone."

Betty became flustered. "You think I'm crazy, don't you?"

"I don't think you're crazy, but I am worried," Kelly said. "It's just... It's not normal."

"Let me ask you something. Do you realize what nerve you and Terry have for doubting this? Both of you believe in God, you believe in heaven, you believe that anything is possible. But this..."

"It's not possible."

"*Why?*" Betty said. "Terry said that with God all things are possible. So why can't he wrap his mind around this? He won't even entertain the possibility that I'm telling the truth. This is..."

"What?"

"Bullshit," blurted Betty.

Betty never cursed, and the colorful language surprised them both.

"I taught high school for nearly forty years," Betty said. "I was above reproach. No one ever questioned my mental state. I was teaching before you were born. I was teaching before that twit Terry was born."

"He's just worried, Mom."

"He's a hypocrite."

"He didn't mean—"

Betty prepared her next words carefully. "He's a hypocrite, and so are you, my dear." And she hung up the telephone and unplugged its cord from the wall.

That night, Betty lay in bed in the darkness, listening to the empty static on the radio. She thought about how Terry had betrayed her, had possibly even betrayed his own faith in God, and about how her Kelly had the nerve to question her mental faculties.

And finally, late that night, Betty drifted off to sleep.

She was awakened just after three by the sound of Bill talking to her through the static.

"Betty," he said.

She sat up, startled. Had she heard something? She tried to clear her mind, to figure out where she was.

"Betty," said Bill again. "Are you there, my dear?"

"Yes," she said, clearing her throat. "I'm here, Bill."

"Are you in bed?"

"Yes, Bill."

"Fine. I've got some time. Just lay back and we can talk in bed like we used to—back when I was still alive...before I got sick."

Betty felt simultaneously overcome with joy and sorrow, and she started to cry again.

"Are you crying, Betty?"

She sniffled, but said nothing.

"You are, aren't you?" asked Bill. "Don't cry old girl. I'm here now."

"Are you?"

"What do you mean? Of course I'm here."

"But are you *really* here?"

"Of course I'm really here, my dear."

"But Terry... I, I... I told Terry..."

"The preacher man?"

"Yes, Terry the preacher."

"You told him about talking to me?"

"Yes."

"You shouldn't have done that, old girl."

"Why?" asked Betty.

"Because he won't be able to hear me," said Bill. "And he won't believe you."

"It's a shame."

"What?"

"A man of God who doesn't believe in miracles."

"Betty, it isn't just that preacher. No one is gonna believe you, dear."

"I guess you're right."

"Did you tell anyone else?"

"Kelly knows."

"*Our* Kelly?" asked Bill.

"Yeah."

"And what does she say?"

"She thinks I'm a crazy old nut. She thinks I need to be locked away in a nursing home."

"She said that?" asked Bill, irritation in his voice.

"No, she didn't come right out and say it, but I know her. That's what's coming next."

Bill said, "No girl of mine is ever gonna be locked away in one of those places. Not if I have anything to do with it."

Betty didn't understand. "What do you mean?"

"I can help you."

"How?"

"Do as I say, old girl."

"Okay. I can do that."

"Unplug the radio."

"Unplug the radio?"

"Yes."

"But how will I talk to you?" Betty asked.

"Don't worry about it. We'll still be able to talk."

"How?"

"I don't know how it works, but we will. That's all I know."

"Okay."

Betty stood up, switched on the lamp next to the bed, and walked over to the radio. She unplugged it.

"You still there, Bill?"

"Yeah."

"Okay, now what?" asked Betty.

"Wrap the cord around the radio and carry it out into the garage."

"Into the garage?"

"Just do it, my dear."

Betty wrapped up the cord and carried the radio through the dark house, through the kitchen, and out into the hot garage.

"Now what, Bill?"

"Get into the car and sit the radio down in the passenger's seat."

"Are you sure?"

"Of course I'm sure," Bill said. "I'm here now, and everything's gonna be okay."

Betty sobbed again. "You promise?"

"I promise, old girl."

"Okay."

Betty climbed into the old car and sat the radio in the passenger's seat. She asked, "Now what?"

"Close the door."

She pulled the car door closed.

"Now start the car and roll down the windows," said Bill.

"Start the car?" Betty asked. "Bill, it's the middle of the night."

"I know what time it is."

Betty looked at the keys dangling from the ignition. "Start the car?"

"Right."

Betty turned the key and started the car. The radio came on, country music spilling out, and she switched it off.

"Roll down the windows," said Bill.

She looked at the radio, unsure.

"You trust me, don't you?'

"Of course I trust you," said Betty.

She rolled down the electric windows.

"Now what?" she asked.

"Recline your seat."

"What for?"

"We're just gonna sit here and talk while the car runs."

Betty thought about it for a moment. "Are you saying what I think you're saying, Bill?"

"I miss you, my dear," he said. "We *all* miss you."

Betty reclined the seat and laid back, her eyelids feeling heavy.

"What do you want to talk about?" she asked.

"You just close your eyes, pretty girl," Bill said. "I'll sing you to sleep, like I did when we first married."

She looked at the radio with momentary unease. She thought about what Bill was asking, and finally she gave in. She laid her head back against the seat and closed her eyes.

Bill started to sing her a lullaby.

She clenched her eyes shut and listened to him.

And she went to sleep to the sound of her husband's soothing voice.

ME AND THE DEVIL BLUES

Robert Johnson saw a shadowy figure in his dream. Robert knew it was a dream, could tell it wasn't waking life, but still found himself feeling afraid. In his dream, Robert was standing about a hundred feet from the big elm tree out near the road at the front of the cotton plantation where he lived. It was nighttime, and the moon was in hiding. The dark, pillowy clouds were moving quickly, but the light of the moon never seemed to break free from behind them. Robert kept his eye on the shadowy figure, standing there beneath the tree. He couldn't see the figure clearly enough to see its movements, but somehow he knew it was motioning to him.

Now feeling unable to control his own bodily functions, Robert felt himself walking through the tall grass as if on auto-pilot, making his way towards the base of the tree. Once Robert was about twenty feet away, the shadowy figure motioned for him to stop. Again Robert couldn't *see* the figure's motions, but he could *feel* them just as sure as he could feel the cool nighttime breeze against his skin.

"Stop," the figure said with a powerful, booming voice. It wasn't a black voice, nor a white voice. This was something else.

Robert stopped, saying nothing, his eyes glued to the figure.

"What do you want?" asked the voice.

And instinctively Robert knew exactly what the voice meant. He answered, "I want to play the guitar. I want to sing the blues."

"Why is this important to you, Robert?" asked the voice, so clear Robert wondered if it was coming from inside his head rather than from the figure.

"All I ever wanted was to play the blues," Robert said. "I mean, I can play the blues, but I want to really be able to *play* the blues. I want to make people dance. I want the sound of my guitar and the sound of my voice to pleasure God."

At this the voice laughed a shrill, eerie laugh.

"What?" asked Robert.

The voice repeated what he'd said mockingly. "*You want to please God?*"

"Yes, sir," Robert said. "I want to please him with the beauty of my music."

"Well then, you've come to the right place."

"Are you God?"

"Heaven's no," the voice said. "Why, you might say I'm the furthest thing from God."

"But you can help me?"

"I'll make you play the guitar like no human has ever played such an instrument. I'll give you the talent to write songs and sing them in a manner that will make God and the angels weep in heaven. You will truly be a power to be reckoned with."

"Why would you do this?"

"It's what I do," said the voice. "It's who I am."

Robert was apprehensive. "And who might that be?"

"I am not God, but you might say I am still the Alpha and the Omega, the yin and the yang, the good and the bad. I am all things, Robert Johnson, and this is what I am here for—to help folks like you fulfill their dreams."

Robert was unsure what to think, but found himself feeling pleased. Soon, if the voice was telling the truth, he would be able to play the blues better than anyone on any of the surrounding plantations. He would be the best of the best.

"What do I need to do?"

"Ah, therein lays the question of all questions, Robert."

"What do you mean?"

"Don't you worry your nappy head about it, son," the voice said. "Just do as I say, and I'll make sure you become the greatest blues singer ever to pick a damned guitar."

"*Ever?*"

"Ever—as in from the past to eternity. No matter what happens, you will always be remembered as the single greatest bluesman of all time. You will have the ability to play the guitar in a manner that seems to make even the strings themselves weep. How does that sound?"

Robert said nothing. He wanted to say it felt good, but he found himself unable to speak. Somehow he knew it wasn't necessary, that the voice already knew his thoughts as quickly as they came to him.

"Listen closely, Robert."

"Okay."

"Here's what you do: next time there's a full moon in the sky, I want you to walk down the old dirt road past the Dockery Plantation. You follow that road several miles into the darkness. It will be a peculiar night, a night made for bargaining. And on that night, you follow that road until you come to a crossroads."

"Okay, then what?"

"Then you wait."

"Wait?" Robert asked. "What for what?"

"Not a *what*," the voice said, "but a *whom*."

"Okay."

"Who will I be waiting for?"

"You will wait there for a man to approach you."

"He be a black man or a white man?"

"On that night, he'll be a black man. He will approach you with a gift."

"A gift?"

"That's right," said the voice. "You tell him what you want and he'll make it happen. All you need is to make sure you take your old guitar with you."

Robert wanted to ask more questions, but the figure disappeared, as did the voice, and daylight pushed out the darkness of the sky and all surroundings. Robert opened his eyes, squinted and shook his head to clear his vision, and found himself awake. And as with most dreams, Robert struggled to remember the details, but this time, unlike the normal ones, they soon returned to him with crystal clarity.

Eleven days passed before a full moon hung in the sky over the plantation. Robert sat out on the porch steps in the darkness, struggling to play something beautiful, Salieri resurrected in the Mississippi Delta. He sat and banged on the guitar with all the fervor and gusto he could sustain, wailing "Crazy Blues." After his rendition of the song, he knew he'd done the best he could possibly do, knowing also that it wasn't good enough. Hell, even Barney, the old hound dog sitting on the porch, hadn't sung along with him.

Robert looked at the moon and knew it was time to begin his journey. He slung his guitar over his shoulder and started walking down the drive towards the old dirt road which passed the plantation. Dockery Plantation, where all the great bluesmen played, was three miles down. Then, the voice had told him, he was to walk another few miles to the crossroads.

At twenty-two, Robert knew enough not to be afraid of the dark. He knew there were no goblins and ghosts and ghoulies hiding in the shadows behind those trees, but what of the shadowy figure from his dream? That had seemed awfully real. If it hadn't been real, then what the hell was

Robert doing making this journey now? It was another breezy night, just as it had been in the dream, and the sounds of owls and other things Robert couldn't instantly identify filled that breeze. The moon was big and full, and it cast light down on the road before him, the overhanging trees leaving menacing shadows in his path. He knew enough not to jump at every sound he heard, but it was difficult finding the restraint.

The voice had been right. There was something peculiar about this night that Robert couldn't put his finger on. It was the kind of night in which nothing surprised you; a dead man might emerge from within those shadows and Robert couldn't say he'd be surprised. Scared to death, sure, but not surprised.

As he walked on, finally approaching the Dockery Plantation, Robert considered strumming his guitar. But he decided against it. It was an eerie night, and he wasn't sure he wanted to invite whatever might be lurking in those shadows out to see him. Also, he wanted to be sure he could hear whatever sounds there were to hear in that darkness.

And he walked.

As he passed the Dockery Plantation, he heard the old bluesmen playing off in the distance, the melancholy sounds of the blues carrying faintly in the breeze. He couldn't make out the songs they played, but he struggled to listen to them anyway, grinning like a madman as he did.

And still he walked further, taking on what felt like another dozen miles. And once his feet hurt to the point where he was sure they were bleeding inside his old shoes, Robert came, at last, to the crossroads—two nondescript dirt roads crossing over one another like a giant crucifix. At almost the very moment he reached the intersection, the breeze picked up, turning into a chilly wind, and that big fat moon slipped behind the clouds.

Robert was afraid.

Play something, came the voice in his head.

No, thought Robert. I won't.

Play something, dammit.

And before he knew what was happening, his fingers began to caress the strings of that old guitar. He half expected to hear himself belt out that old ditty with a passion and talent he had not possessed previously, but this didn't happen. Instead, he played "Crazy

Blues" with all the mediocrity with which he had played it before. And as he did so, he heard himself wailing off-key, and Robert felt his heart sink in his chest, knowing he was no better than he had been.

He stopped playing and looked down at the dusty road.

"Hello, Robert," came a deep voice from behind.

Robert turned quickly, seeing a large black man standing there, dressed to the nines, fedora in hand. He put his hand out for Robert to shake. "You can call me Mr. Scratch." Robert slowly moved his hand out towards the man's, taking it in his own and shaking it.

"What would you like?" Mr. Scratch asked.

Robert felt the words rising up from his throat. "I want to play the blues."

Mr. Scratch chuckled. "The blues are a mighty powerful thing, Robert. You sure you've got what it takes to be a bonafide blues man?"

Robert was unsure how to answer the question. "No, I'm not. I was hoping you could help me develop that...whatever it is that it takes to be a bonafide blues man."

"No worries," Mr. Scratch said. "I can do that. Why, I can make you the greatest blues man ever to pick up a guitar. I can give you the ability to write a song that'll make the hardest men weep like infants. I can give you the voice of the angels—a voice so beautiful that it touches a man's soul in a place where normal music don't. I'll make you the greatest ever."

"I want that," Robert said. "I want that very badly."

"Do you know what a pact is?"

Robert tried to process these foreign-sounding words, but had no clue what in the hell they meant. For all he knew, Mr. Scratch could have been speaking French.

"What it means," the man said, "is that you and I will make a deal that will be unlike any you have ever made in all your life."

"Okay."

"It means I will give you five years from now in which you will be the greatest blues man ever to play the music. In return, I will collect your mortal soul. Do you know what that means?"

Robert considered this for a moment. This time Mr. Scratch didn't interrupt him with the answer. "It means you're gonna make me the greatest blues singer of all time for five years," Robert said.

"And?"

"You're gonna come and take away my soul in five years."

"Yes, Robert," Mr. Scratch said. "Five years from this very night."

"Five years from *tonight*?"

"Yes."

"I'll die?"

"Unn-huh."

"And go to Hell?"

"Ain't nobody forcing you to make this deal, Robert," the man said. "You can take it or leave it, but if you want to be the greatest blues singer who ever lived, you'll take it. You're only gonna get one opportunity to make this deal. Do you understand?"

"Yes, sir."

"You got any questions, Robert?"

"Hell...is it as bad as they say?"

"No," Mr. Scratch said. "It's far worse."

"But I'll be the greatest bluesman in all of Mississippi if I make the deal?"

The man laughed. "You'll be the greatest bluesman in the *world*, from Memphis to Tokyo, Japan."

Robert was ready to make the agreement. "Where do I sign?"

"Hand me your guitar," Mr. Scratch said. "Let me tighten the strings."

Robert handed over the old guitar and allowed the man to tune it. The man tweaked the strings for a moment and handed it back. "Play something for me," said Mr. Scratch. "Play something beautiful."

Robert took the guitar in his hands, finding that it now fit in his grip in a familiar manner in which it never had before. He started to strum the guitar, singing a new song, "Me and the Devil Blues," which came to him instantly, fully-formed. And as he played, Mr. Scratch clapped along and stomped his foot in time with the music.

Just as Robert finished the song, automobile headlights approached from the opposite direction from which he had come. The automobile, a black Model T, pulled up, stopping beside them. There was no one inside. Mr. Scratch opened the door and climbed in behind the wheel.

"Mr. Scratch," Robert said. "I know you don't owe me nothing else, but I was wondering if I could catch a ride up to Ruleville."

"You wanna try out your new-found skill?"

"Yes, sir."

"Climb in, boy."

"You sure you don't mind?"

"Hell no, it's the least I can do, son."

Robert climbed inside the Model T, and he and Mr. Scratch roared off down the road, kicking up dust as they went.

When Mr. Scratch and Robert arrived in Ruleville, they pulled up in front of a colored blues club called Bunny's.

"Here you go," Mr. Scratch said.

"This a good place?"

"Ah, son, this is the *best* place."

Robert climbed out of the Model T, took his old guitar with him, and thanked Mr. Scratch for the ride.

"Pleasure's all mine, son," Mr. Scratch said, tipping the brim of his fedora.

Robert turned and walked towards the entrance. When he got to the door, he turned to wave to Mr. Scratch, but there was no one there. Robert shrugged and pulled the door open, the sounds of the blues slapping him in the face as he did.

A man approached him from inside. "You play?"

"I'm the best there is," Robert said.

The man laughed. "That's a mighty tall boast. We get the best from all over Mississippi in here." The man turned to an associate, pointing to Robert. "Kid says he's the best."

Finally, when the man onstage was finished playing his song, they led Robert up to the stage. Robert found himself a stool, raised his guitar, and played the best damned blues anyone in Bunny's could ever recall having heard.

THE TIRE KING OF INDIANA

Dana Gottlieb hadn't had this much fun since the time he'd banged two escorts in a Volvo parked behind Treasure Island in Vegas. There was still alcohol involved, but this was a much less decadent occasion. Dana's best friend from high school, Dustin Farmer, had come to Los Angeles to visit. The two old pals had spoken with one another about once a year, but they hadn't seen each other in the flesh since college. That had been a couple decades ago now, time flying like a motherfucker.

It was three in the morning, and the two middle-aged men had been partying hard ever since Dustin's plane had landed at LAX that afternoon. Dana had drunk the better part of two bottles of cognac, and Dustin had polished off a twelver of Bud Light by himself.

"Well, shit, I'm drunk," Dustin announced. "Now what?"

"I think I have just the thing for the occasion," Dana said, going to his bedroom and rooting around in his gym bag. He produced a nice big baggy of coke, and brought it back out to his friend. "I've got this," he said, shaking the baggy between his thumb and forefinger.

"Is that what I think it is?" Dustin asked.

"Depends on what you think it is."

"Is it coke?"

Dana laughed. "It ain't baking powder."

And within ninety seconds the two of them were taking turns snorting lines of coke off Dana's glass table with hundred dollar bills. This went on for another fifteen minutes. Finally they took a break.

"That's good shit," Dustin said.

"That's all I get."

"Man, I haven't done coke since college."

"You're shitting me."

Dustin said, "I shit you not. I did crank twice, but I haven't done blow in twenty years."

"You've been missing out," Dana said. "You're living a sorely inadequate existence, my friend. I couldn't manage without a line or two a day."

"You do that much?"

"Sure I do," Dana said. "Everyone in the record industry does."

"Man, no one in the travel-guide-writing business does," Dustin said, laughing at his own joke.

"That's too bad."

"I guess. But you know, I've been married for a long time."

"I tried that noise," Dana said. "Twice."

"And?"

"It didn't take."

Dustin laughed. "Marriage is hard work, man. I have one of the best marriages around, and we still fight all the goddamn time."

"You do?"

"Oh, yeah," Dustin said. "Does a bear shit in the woods and wipe his ass with a fluffy white rabbit?"

Dana chuckled, going to the table to do another line.

"You know what the problem with coke is?" asked Dana.

"What?"

"The high doesn't last long enough."

Dustin nodded. "True. The two times I tried crank, I was high for a really long time."

"But it wasn't a *pure* high."

"Yeah, but it was a high. Being high is like getting head—high is high is high is high."

Dana laughed. "Don't be looking at me for head, because I don't go that way."

"I was just saying that a crank high lasts a hell of a lot longer than a coke high."

"But it's the difference between a can of Milwaukee's Best and a bottle of *Courvoisier*." Dana said, bending down to snort a line. When he sat up, there were white crystals stuck to his nostril.

Dustin motioned towards them. "You've got coke on your nose, Scarface."

Dana wiped off his nose.

"So you've got a pretty good marriage?" Dana asked.

"Things are good. You know, I can't complain. I mean, I could, but who would give a shit?"

Dana raised his bottle of cognac. "Not me."

"But you know, it's not so bad. We don't have sex very often, but it's a good life. We're like a team."

Dana thought that sounded boring as fuck—especially the no-sex part—but didn't say anything.

"Being married is like being in a partnership," Dustin said. "An actual, legit partnership."

"Okay, if someone offered you a million dollars to sleep with your wife, would you let 'em?"

"You got a million dollars?"

Dana laughed. "No, but what if I did?"

"Then I'd probably say yes. It's not that I wouldn't care, but man, we got bills to pay and those fuckers don't pay themselves. We've got a mortgage and college tuition... It would be nice to be able to breathe for a while without creditors calling every five minutes."

"So you'd let someone bang your wife for a million bucks?"

"Dude," Dustin said. "I'd let someone bang *me* for a million bucks. Gladly. If there was a way to turn all this bullshit around within the span of a day or so, I'd do whatever it took."

Dana nodded. "I understand."

"You do?"

"Sure. Now do another line of coke."

"Don't mind if I do," Dustin said, going to the table and helping himself.

The conversation returned to women, just as it always had with them.

"I'm sure glad I didn't marry Tara," Dustin said.

"You dodged a bullet there."

"No shit."

"She was as crazy as crazy comes."

"Oh, yeah. She was a goddamn loon."

"Just imagine if I'd had a kid with her."

"Again, you dodged the bullet."

"I can't believe she had an abortion and didn't tell me."

"I know you felt like shit about the whole thing," Dana said, "but honestly, would you have wanted to have had a kid with her?"

"Well, no..."

"Just imagine how miserable that kid's life would have been," Dana said. "Truth be told, she did that kid a favor."

Dustin rubbed his chin. "I guess."

"You guess, shit. She would have made that *Mommy Dearest* chick seem like Mother of the Goddamn Year."

"Yeah," Dustin said. "You ever talk to any of your ex-girlfriends?"

"I'm friends with some of them on Facebook, but I try my best not to talk to any of 'em."

"Wise policy."

"Do you talk to either of your ex-wives?"

"As little as possible," Dana said. "One I'm free and clear of, but the other, well, we got a kid, you know, so I have to deal with her on occasion."

"How's that go?"

Dana chuckled, taking a swig of the cognac. "Pretty much how you'd think it would."

Dustin laughed. "That good, huh?"

"She married some schmuck, a lawyer, and she makes our son call him 'daddy.' So that's a good time. And of course she moved halfway across the country so I couldn't see the kid."

"But she still expects child support every month?"

"You kidding me?" Dana asked. "Man, if her child support shows up even a day late, she's on the phone chewing my ass out."

"Do you miss your kid?"

"Not as much as I wish I did."

Dustin made a confused face. "Which means?"

"Which means he's an asshole just like his mom. He thinks she's the most awesome thing ever to happen on this Earth, and he thinks I'm a loser."

"Why?"

"Because his mother tells him that shit," Dana said. He looked over to the table. "I think I'm ready for some more blow." He went to the table and started setting up a couple more lines.

Dustin asked, "You ever miss Indiana?"

"Oh, god, no," Dana said. "I don't miss anything about that stupid little town. I hated Avery, and high school was the worst four years of my life, hands down."

"I didn't think it was so bad," said Dustin.

Dana laughed.

"What?" Dustin asked.

"It's because you're in denial. You like to pretend you were on the bubble of the popular kids. But that ain't the truth, Dusty. The truth is that we were both a couple of dorks who didn't fit in with the so-called cool kids. So what? It is what it is. I've had a good life. I don't need the approval of a bunch of stupid jackasses who don't know shit about the real world."

"We weren't *that* unpopular," Dustin said.

"Just keep telling yourself that."

"I didn't think it was that bad."

"Maybe I had higher expectations than you did."

"Maybe," Dustin said, taking a swig of his beer. "But why does that sound backhanded to me?"

"Take it as you will."

"Well," Dustin said, "what was so bad about high school to you?"

"The awfulness of my high school years has a single name."

"What do you mean?"

"Jake Kellerman."

Dustin nodded. "Yeah, that guy was a dick."

"He single-handedly ruined everything I ever gave a shit about," Dana said. Then he added, "What would you say if I told you I killed him?"

"What do you mean?"

"He's dead. I killed him."

Dustin was confused. "What the fuck are you talking about?"

"I got his head inside my bowling bag. You wanna see it?"

An awkward silence settled in between them. Dustin was drunk and stoned enough he wasn't sure if Dana was serious.

"Are you for real?"

"Of course I didn't kill him, dumbass," Dana said. "But of course I *wish* he was dead. I haven't wanted anyone dead that badly since Al Davis and maybe, *maybe*, Bin-Laden."

Dustin chuckled.

"No, I'm serious," Dana said. "I hate that guy with every fiber of my being. He doesn't deserve to live."

"You know, I've heard he's fairly successful now," said Dustin. "Nice house, pretty wife, lots of money."

Great! thought Dana. *Just what I wanted to hear!*

"Successful how?" Dana asked.

"I'm not sure. He owns his own business, I know that. It seems like it was tires or something like that... Something auto-related. I can't remember. But I heard he has a nice, big house and that he drives a Maserati."

"I hate that."

"What?"

"It's not fair. A piece of shit like Jake Kellerman doesn't deserve to be successful."

"What do you care? You're pretty successful yourself."

Dana looked around. "What are you talking about? I'm *very* successful. Much more than some asshole Tire King of Indiana. I've worked with some of the biggest bands in music. Christ, I worked with Paul McCartney. *I worked with a fucking Beatle!* Do you understand what that means? I worked with Michael Jackson. I got drunk with Lou Reed once. I did an eight ball and shared a hooker with Keith Richards. *Keith fucking Richards!*"

"It's not a big deal," Dustin said. "Don't get bent out of shape. I didn't mean he was more successful than you. Shit, you're both more successful than I am."

"I worked with the Beach Boys. Do you get what that means? *The freaking Beach Boys!*"

"I didn't mean anything."

"If there's one saving grace, it's that he didn't marry Kimmie."

"What do you mean?"

Dana grinned. "Last I heard she was a lesbian."

"Apparently she changed her mind," Dustin said.

"What does that mean?"

"It means they're married."

And that's when Dana *really* lost it.

"That fucker isn't good enough for Kimmie Godfrey! It isn't fair!"

"I know you liked her and all, but come on, you know she was out of your league."

"But *he* wasn't?"

"Well," Dustin said, "he was the captain of the football team, he could sing, he was popular...he was one of the most popular people in high school."

"Shut up."

"What?"

Dana repeated himself. "Just shut up and drink the beer I bought you. Do some more of my coke. I don't wanna talk about Jake Kellerman anymore."

"I'm sorry," Dustin said. "I had no idea it was such a touchy subject."

"Just do some fucking coke and shut up."

A couple days passed, and Dana found his thoughts returning more and more frequently to Jake Kellerman. He was obsessed. He couldn't get the sorry son of a bitch out of his head. He kept thinking back to all his most embarrassing moments in high school and seeing Jake Kellerman as being the single common denominator.

He remembered the time he finally got up the nerve to ask Janie Cosgrove to prom. He was leaning against the locker next to hers, trying his best to act cool, to flirt with this girl who was only a tad bit out of his league. Both of them were laughing and she was clearly enjoying his company. Things were going well, and he knew she knew what he wanted, and yet there she was, sticking around. Things were going so well, and then Jake Kellerman had shown up, pouring the remainder of a chewing tobacco spit cup over his head. Before Dana could respond, Jake had then shoved his head hard into the wall. Dana had fallen to the ground, still in shock and not fully aware of what was happening, with Janie Cosgrove standing over him—*laughing*.

She, along with everyone else in that hallway, had laughed. Dana no longer remembered what he'd done next, but guessed he'd probably scurried away in tears. And that was the end of his conversations with Janie

Cosgrove; she never spoke to him again. He wound up asking a little crippled girl to the prom instead, and she and her family had literally moved away on prom day. Seriously. That happened. Her whole goddamn family up and moved away, god knows why, and Dana wound up watching a *Star Trek* marathon at home by himself.

The following year, Dana was in a serious relationship with a freshman girl named Yolanda Evans. They went to the homecoming dance together, and it was like something out of a bad movie—his average-looking girlfriend revealed herself to be a real knock-out when she put on makeup and dressed up. Dana had gone to that dance with Yolanda, feeling as proud as a boy could feel. She was drop-dead gorgeous, and everyone at the dance stared at her with their mouths agape, wondering who the hell she was. And then, of course, Jake Kellerman showed up and took her away. Never mind the fact that he was there with Kimmie Godfrey, the most beautiful girl in school. Jake had taken Yolanda to the gymnasium, where'd she gladly dropped to her knees and given him a blow job.

If there was an upside, it was that Jake hadn't beat Dana up at the dance in addition to stealing his girlfriend and poking his dick in her mouth. But Jake being Jake, it didn't end there. Once they got back to school the following Monday, he went out of his way to mock Dana, saying things like, "Hey, where's your girlfriend? I could use some head." Jake Kellerman was a real class act.

And those hadn't been the only incidents involving Jake. No, there had been countless occurrences of him randomly slamming Dana into the walls or punching him in the face over the years. But there were just too many of those to recount in detail, and the truth was that they all kind of blurred together.

And here they were now, more than twenty years after those incidents, and Dana still found himself hating Jake more than he could possibly put into words. He was now fully aware—*how could he not be?*—that all that stuff with Jake had changed him forever. Every accomplishment he'd had in his life, every hey-look-at-me moment he'd enjoyed, had been a direct response to the bullying of Jake Kellerman. And those successes were never enough. He always found himself wanting to accomplish more, *needing* to accomplish more, to silence the Jake Kellerman voice that followed him around, existing somewhere deep down inside his own psyche.

He now realized that he'd never been free of the bastard. Jake Kellerman had bullied so many people that he probably didn't even remember Dana anymore, and yet here was Dana living his life by an impossible standard that had been set and defined by the "cool" kids, i.e. Jake. He did drugs because he hated himself. Why did he hate himself? Jake Kellerman. He'd cheated on every woman he'd ever dated because he felt the need to prove himself. Why? Jake Kellerman.

And now Dana realized for the first time what he should have seen two decades before—that he would never be free as long as Jake Kellerman was still walking the Earth, still breathing air into his lungs, still existing.

Dana knew what had to be done.

Jake Kellerman had to go.

Dana did some research and found that Jake and Kimmie were still living in the same crappy little burg in which they'd all grown up together. Dana hadn't been back to Avery in more than twenty years, and he now saw that Jake Kellerman was the primary reason for that. Here he'd been angry at the entire town all these years, and he now knew that it had really been Jake alone he should have been upset with. Sure, the other kids laughed when Jake had hurt and/or humiliated him, and sure no one stepped up to his defense, but in the Grand Guignol known as high school this was to be expected; everyone was miserable, and they all enjoyed witnessing each other's pain.

So here was Dana, finally going home, and he only had plans to see his arch-enemy Jake Kellerman. His plane had landed a hundred miles away in Indianapolis, and he'd then rented a Mitsubishi to drive to Avery. He was now driving in the pouring rain towards the small town, would arrive at roughly two a.m., and planned to be back out of Avery before anyone knew he'd even been there.

The rain was beating down so hard the windshield wipers could barely keep up, and lightning kept flashing across the sky, followed by large burps of thunder. It was as dramatic a night for Jake Kellerman's exit as Dana could have imagined, and he loved it. He felt a mixture of excitement and cocaine surging through his body, and he shivered a bit despite the heater being on. Nervous and enthusiastic, he could find no music that suited his mood, so he chose to drive with the radio off, just listening to the sounds of the rain and the windshield wipers.

He hadn't been this amped about anything in years. He couldn't believe he'd never considered killing Jake Kellerman prior to his little joke, and he found that the idea suited him. It was a lived-in idea that had probably sat dormant somewhere deep in the recesses of his mind for many years without his knowing and he now found that it fit him like a glove. If there was anything that gave him pause, it was the thought of having to deal with Jake's wife, Kimmie, with whom Dana had always had a bit of an obsession, and their two children, ages five and nine. But they were just collateral damage. These things couldn't be helped, Dana supposed. It was worth it. You wanna take out Hitler, you're gonna lose a few officers along the way. That's just the way it was.

When Dana finally got to Avery, he could see, even through the rain and darkness, that the little shit hole had changed for the worse. There were a couple of new businesses he didn't recognize, but there were a whole lot more old businesses now closed down. The town was like Jake Kellerman—on the verge of death.

Dana found Jake's house easily, as he remembered the once-new street it sat upon. It was a huge goddamn house, as gaudy as you like, a small-town Indiana version of a baby mansion. It was a newish house, had probably been built specifically for Jake and Kimmie, and had thin white pillars on its porch, supporting the roof.

Dammit, Dana thought. He really hated to see Jake Kellerman doing this well for himself, even if he was about die.

There was only one car—a red Maserati—parked in the drive. Dana hoped this meant the wife was away, but then feared she might return in the middle of the act. Dana parked behind the sports car. He then slipped on his leather gloves, gathered up everything he would need for his little visit with the Tire King, and climbed out of the Mitsubishi into the rain.

He walked slowly and calmly towards the front door, wiping his shoes on the big WELCOME FRIENDS mat on the porch. He pushed the little orange-lit button and rang the doorbell. He then removed the .38 from his waistband and held it at his side. He couldn't hear anything inside as any sounds were muffled by the din of the falling rain. After about a minute, he considered ringing the bell again, but then saw a dark silhouette inside the little stained-glass window. The door opened.

And there he was—Jake Kellerman, in the flesh. He looked a little bit older, bald and ridiculously muscular, hunched over like a fucking troglodyte. He was rubbing his eyes. "Do you know what time it is?"

Dana raised the pistol. "I believe I do."

"What the hell?"

"Why don't you let me in, Jake old buddy. We got a lot of catching up to do."

Jake squinted. "Do I know you?"

Dana used the gun to push his way in, and Jake backed into the dining room.

"What is this, a home invasion?" Jake asked.

Dana grinned. "No. Just a little reunion between old friends."

Jake still had no clue who he was.

They played a game of twenty questions, with Jake trying to figure out where he knew him from, while Dana duct-taped him to a dining room chair.

"I'm gonna fuck you up when I get out of this," Jake said.

Dana smiled broadly. "Now there's the Jake Kellerman we all know and love."

"Who are you?"

"I got a question for *you*—where are your wife and kids?"

Jake didn't flinch. "They went to Akron."

"What the fuck is in Akron?"

"My wife and kids," Jake said smugly.

"Ah, funny man!" Dana backhanded him across the face with the .38, and a bloody tooth flew from his mouth.

"I'm gonna..."

Dana looked Jake in the eyes. "You're not gonna do shit. Now really, why are your wife and kids in Akron?"

"They're visiting my wife's sister," Jake said, looking annoyed. "Who are you?"

"Just some guy you fucked over years ago."

Jake chuckled. "You're gonna have to be more specific."

"I'm glad to hear you take pride in being a jackass."

"So what'd I do to you? Was it in high school? College? At work, *what?*"

"It wasn't work," Dana said. "It was personal."

Jake laughed again. "What'd I do, fuck your wife?"

"Close."

Dana smacked Jake with the .38 again. This time he wasn't trying to be tough—it was reflexive. *We've got a long way to go here*, Dana thought to himself. *Let's not get carried away and finish him off before we're ready.*

Dana noticed a pack of Pall Malls and a nudie-girl lighter on the table.

"You smoke?" Dana asked.

"Hey, we all got a few bad habits."

Dana picked up the pack and looked back at Jake. "You got more than a few, buddy."

Dana put a cigarette to his lips and lit it, drew on it, and blew the smoke out at Jake.

"Can I have one?" Jake asked.

"I don't know. These things'll kill you, you know."

Jake didn't like not getting his way. *"Just give me a goddamn cigarette!"*

Dana moved forward. "Your wish is my command." As Dana approached Jake's face with the lit cigarette, he considered burning out his eye, but thought the better of it. After all, that would just stop their conversation cold. So instead he just burned a little round hole on Jake's cheekbone. It hissed a little as it burrowed itself into soft flesh. Jake buckled hard in the tape and let out a scream.

"We can't have that," Dana said. He stretched out a length of tape, tearing it off, and then wrapped it around Jake's mouth. He made a point to brush against the cigarette wound as he did. Jake jolted in agony, his screams muffled behind the tape.

"You said you wanted a cigarette," Dana said.

Jake tried to talk through the tape. *"Unggh! Ooonk! Oooh!"*

Jake put the pistol up to Jake's head, placing its tip against his forehead.

"You're not so tough now, are you?"

"Ooong! Ungggh!"

"I really want you to guess who I am, but I can't do it with tape over your mouth. I'll take it off if you'll promise to keep it down a bit."

Jake nodded. "Nnnnngg!"

Dana removed the tape, and Jake gasped for air.

"Okay, who am I?"

Jake stared at him blankly. "I don't know. Gimme a hint."

"We went to high school together."

"We did?"

"Yeah."

"Okay, gimme another clue."

"My girlfriend gave you head."

Jake had no clue. "I dunno."

"It was at homecoming. She blew you in the gym and then you went home with Kimmie."

Jake still didn't know.

"What?!" Dana asked. "How the fuck can you not remember *that?*"

"I banged almost every girl in the school. How am I supposed to remember all of 'em?"

Dana didn't know how to react. He'd wanted Jake to remember him, to remember what he'd done, and maybe even feel some remorse. But no, that had been too much to hope for.

"What else?"

"You used to beat me up all the time."

Jake grinned. *"Really?* That doesn't narrow it down. I beat up *everyone* in high school. I even beat up Mr. Johnson, the Civics teacher."

"Dana."

"What?"

"My name is Dana."

Jake stared at him blankly. *"Dana?"*

"Dana Gottlieb."

"I don't remember you at all."

And now Dana saw that what he had hoped to accomplish here was a lost cause. It was the same old thing; no matter what he accomplished, it would never be enough, always because of Jake.

"I've hated you for the past twenty years, and you don't even remember me?"

Jake laughed at him. "Shows how much you meant to me."

"No one meant anything to you."

"What do you mean?"

"Kimmie."

"I love Kimmie."

"But you cheat on her."

"That doesn't mean I don't love her."

"You beat her up when we were in high school."

Jake looked irritated. "Fuck do you care?"

"You did it at school...in Home Ec class," Dana said. "She was pregnant with your baby. She lost it because of you."

"Look, man, I'm tired of this. Do whatever you're gonna do here and get it over with."

Dana reached into his duffel bag and pulled out a power drill, sitting it on the dining room table. Then he reached into the bag and brought out a handsaw, sitting it beside the drill.

Jake's eyes got big. "What are you gonna do?"

"I'm gonna hurt you. Real bad."

Jake tried to act tough. "Just do it."

"You and I are gonna flip a coin, Jake."

"For what?"

Dana pulled out a quarter. "Heads you get the power drill, tails you get the saw." And he flipped the coin. "Call it in the air, Jake."

"Tails," Jake managed.

Dana caught the coin and slapped it against the back of his hand, looking at it. He looked up and grinned. "Today's your lucky day."

It was just before eight when Dana boarded the Delta flight from Indianapolis to Los Angeles. The rain had subsided outside, and it was looking like it was going to be a beautiful, sunny day.

Dana slowly made his way down the aisle towards his seat, moving as briskly as he could amidst the herd of human cattle. He overheard someone talking about politics. Another woman was saying she couldn't wait to get home to see her grandchildren. Another man was complaining about how small the seats were on the flight.

Once Dana found his seat, he opened the luggage compartment overhead, but found that it was full. He looked at his bag.

"Do you want me to take that for you, sir?" asked a stewardess.

"No," Dana said. "I just have this one small bag. I'll just keep it with me."

And he sat down in his seat, sliding his brown bowling bag beneath him.

An elderly woman took the seat beside him. "Are you having a nice day?" she asked.

Dana smiled. "The best. Simply the best."

THE SOUTH WILL RISE AGAIN

It was a warm mid-March evening, and the guys were flying down a Tennessee back road in Wilson's new 1968 Cadillac Eldorado. They were having the time of their lives. The three of them—Cleavon, Marshall, and Wilson—were driving from American Baptist College in Nashville down to Atlanta for spring break. The radio station they were listening to was breaking up, George Jones starting to bleed through, and Marshall turned the knob. "I'm not listening to any of that hillbilly cracker music," he said, twisting the knob until he found James Brown howling "I Feel Good."

"Now *that's* music," said Marshall.

"How many girls you think are gonna be there?" Cleavon asked.

"In Atlanta?" Wilson asked. "Lots of girls, man. More than you can even imagine. It's gonna be black girl heaven, with fine-looking sisters everywhere, as far as the eye can see."

Cleavon grinned. "Sounds good to me."

"Don't it?" said Marshall.

"Why are there so many black girls in Atlanta?" Cleavon asked.

Marshall said, "Morehouse is there, and there are a whole bunch of black colleges within a day's drive. Where else are they gonna go for spring break?"

"I might just catch me a woman to settle down with," Marshall joked.

Wilson chuckled. "You'll be lucky to catch crabs."

Marshall thought about that. "You had crabs before?"

"No, but my friend Jerry had 'em once."

"Were they bad?"

"Well, they weren't good. But he said they weren't really as bad as you might think. More of a pain than anything. He had to shave off all his pubic hair and put on some kind of ointment down there."

"And that killed 'em?"

"Deader than a Kennedy."

"Hmmm," Marshall said. "I think I'll just use a rubber."

This made Cleavon and Wilson laugh.

Cleavon said, "Good policy."

"Besides, there are all kinds of things you can catch having sex these days," Wilson said. "I hear brothers are comin' back from Vietnam with all kinds of crazy shit from having sex with those Vietnamese girls. And now all that nasty shit's here, too. So yeah, wearin' a rubber's the way to go. Besides, you don't wanna have a baby at nineteen."

Marshall chuckled. "You're right there. I'm not ready to be a father. Maybe one day, but not now. There's still a lot of stuff I want to do before I settle down."

"Like what?" asked Cleavon.

"I wanna go to Paris. I wanna see the champs-elysees. I wanna write a novel."

"You wanna write a novel?" asked Cleavon.

"I wanna write a *bunch* of novels."

"What kind of novels?"

Marshall said, "Whatever kinds I feel like. Look at Gordon Parks."

"*The Learning Tree*," said Wilson. "That's a good one."

"I wanna go to Paris and write about being a black man abroad," Marshall said.

Cleavon nodded. "Yeah, I could see that. Kind of a fish-out-of-water thing."

"And think of all the Parisian women you could have sex with over there," Wilson said.

Cleavon chuckled. "Leave it to you to bring the conversation back around to sex."

"I hear those white women over there like black men," said Wilson. "Have you *seen* those French women? Man, they look fine as hell. They look better than American models, and that's just their normal, every day girls."

Cleavon put his hand up for Wilson, who smacked it with a five.

"You tell me when you're goin' to Paris, I just might go with you," said Wilson. "We'll be a couple of uppity brothers, writin' novels and screwin' Parisian women."

Cleavon looked at Wilson. "You're gonna write a novel, too?"

Wilson said, "I'm gonna be the black Mickey Spillane!"

Marshall laughed. "Sounds like a plan."

The James Brown record ended, and a Nancy Sinatra song came on.

"Turn off that noise," said Marshall.

"Nah," Cleavon said. "Leave it on. That's my girl, Nancy Sinatra."

"What're you talkin' about, Nancy Sinatra?" asked Wilson.

"Have you *seen* Nancy Sinatra?" Cleavon asked.

Wilson nodded. "She's got a nice, round ass on her."

"So because she's got a nice ass," Marshall said, "we've gotta sit here and listen to her crap music? You know, she's not here. She's not giving out head to anyone who can make it all the way through her awful goddamn song."

"You don't like it?" asked Cleavon.

"Hell no!" said Wilson. "I'd rather hear your dumb ass sing."

So Cleavon started singing the Nancy Sinatra song.

"Oh, man," Wilson said. "I shoulda known."

The three of them roared with laughter.

Marshall asked, "What would you do if *you* got a girl pregnant?"

"I'd take her back home to see Doc Sonny and get fixed," said Wilson.

"Doc Sonny?"

"Yeah. He's a veterinarian by day, and he gives women 'the operation' at night."

"You sound like you know all about it," Marshall said.

"Maybe I do," Wilson said. "When I was seventeen, I got this girl named Dorothy Carter pregnant. I knew if I told my father, he'd skin my hide. And if her mean old grandmother found out—boy, there would have been hell to pay!"

"So she got it taken care of?" asked Marshall.

Wilson nodded.

Cleavon asked, "Do you ever feel bad about it?"

"I try not to think about it," Wilson said. "I'm not exactly happy about it, but when I think about it, I ask myself where my life would be today if I'd had a baby with that girl."

"And where's that?"

"I'd be working in that factory right there alongside my father, and that's no life at all. I've watched him work his fingers to the bone all these years, and it's killing him. He's gonna dead before he's fifty. And do you think anybody at that factory cares? Hell no. They'll just get someone else to take his place before he's even cold and in the ground."

Cleavon lit a cigarette, and the pungent odor of smoke filled the car.

"Dammit, man," said Wilson. "The least you could do is roll down the goddamn window when you're gonna smoke."

Cleavon rolled down the window, but said nothing.

Marshall turned to Wilson. "So you're meeting your girl in Atlanta, huh?"

Wilson grinned. "Yes, sir. Me and Mary Lou are gonna have a good old time."

"How long's it been since you saw her last?" asked Cleavon.

"Almost a year." Wilson now had a photograph of her out and was kissing it.

"Man," Cleavon said, "you don't bring your girl to spring break. Don't you know anything?"

Wilson laughed.

"It's like taking a bologna sandwich to an all-you-can-eat buffet," said Marshall. "That shit doesn't make any sense."

Wilson's eyes narrowed. "You callin' my Mary Lou a bologna sandwich?"

"Yes, I am," said Marshall. "She's a damned good-lookin' bologna sandwich, but you can have her any time. Spring break is for meeting new girls. Man, I thought I taught you better. You're disappointing me, son."

"You guys can have all the crabs and Vietnamese diseases," Wilson said. "I'll be just fine with my Mary Lou."

The Nancy Sinatra song ended, and Sam and Dave came bursting onto the radio singing "Soul Man."

"Now that's my song right there," Cleavon said. "Why don't you turn that shit up a little bit?"

"Don't mind if I do," said Wilson, turning up the volume. The sounds of "Soul Man" now filled the automobile, and each of the three men snapped their fingers and danced in their seats.

Cleavon said, "They should make more music like this."

Marshall nodded. "They should definitely do that."

Then, out of the blue, the song went off and an announcer interrupted. "We are getting reports that..."

"What the fuck?" asked Cleavon. "I really wanted to hear that."

"Quiet," said Wilson. "I wanna hear this."

The reporter said, "large groups of what appear to be walking corpses attacking and killing residents in Pittsburgh, Pennsylvania. We have received reports of these incidents from all across the country now, from Los Angeles to New York City. At this time, government officials are unable to speculate on the cause of this outbreak, but promise to keep us posted as new details emerge. I repeat, large groups of people appearing to be walking corpses are attacking people and killing them. Most of Atlanta is shut down, and the city has issued an alert. Local authorities are asking travelers not to try and enter the city. Residents of Atlanta are asked to stay inside their homes until the threat can be contained."

"Do you think it's real?" asked Wilson.

"It's on the radio," said Marshall.

"Yeah," Wilson said, "but so was that *War of the Worlds* thing."

"Go ahead and turn it," Cleavon said. "See what they're saying on other stations."

Wilson turned the knob and changed the channel. Soon an old, white, southern minister came over the radio. "This is it," he said. "The rapture is upon us. Our Lord Jesus Christ is coming back to take his followers to the Promised Land..."

"Different station," said Cleavon.

Wilson turned the knob again, and a country-western station came on. He continued turning the knob, and the next station was saying basically the same thing as the first had.

"Shit," Marshall said. "What do you think it's all about?"

"Well, I know what I *don't* believe it is," Wilson said. "I don't believe it's corpses walking around killing people. That sounds like a load of horse shit to me."

Cleavon said, "Agreed."

"Maybe it's Communists," said Marshall.

"Or maybe aliens," said Cleavon, getting in on the joke.

Marshall added, "It's those damn Vietcong."

"So really, what do we do now?" Cleavon asked.

"I think we've got to go to Atlanta," said Wilson. "We've got nowhere else to go. Besides, everything looks completely normal out here. It can't really be all that bad. I mean, if I saw hordes of crazy people walking around out here, I might be inclined to believe that something's going on. But I haven't seen shit."

"I don't know," said Marshall. "The radio said—"

"The radio said there were dead people walking around killing people," Cleavon said. "And dead people don't do anything. They're just dead. So who cares what that damned thing says?"

"I've got a bad feeling about this," Marshall said.

"Well, where would you wanna go?" Wilson asked. "I mean, we're out here in the middle of nowhere. We at least have to drive until we reach a town with a motel."

Cleavon said, "I hope they've got a pool."

Marshall rolled his eyes. "I hope they don't have any walking dead people. That's what I hope."

Wilson nodded. "Yeah. That would be good, too."

"But a pool," Cleavon said. "I could definitely go for a swim right about now."

"Yeah," Marshall said. "I say we stop at the next motel and stay there until we find out what the hell is going on."

They drove until they reached the next town, Dead Possum, which was a rundown little bit of nothingness that fully lived up to the expectations set by its moniker. The town seemed to have nothing more than a few houses and a filling station. But there was no motel and no walking corpses to be seen. There were also no people anywhere in sight.

"Well," Marshall said. "We might as well stop and stretch our legs. We need gas anyway."

The others agreed, and Marshall turned the Eldorado into the lot of the filling station, pulling up in front of the pumps. They waited several minutes, but no attendant came out. Finally, they approached the station itself, but found that the building was locked up and there was no one around.

"Shit," Marshall said. "We really need gas."

"Any idea how far it is to the next town?" asked Wilson.

"No idea."

"I guess there's no reason to stay here."

"Guess not," said Marshall.

They climbed back into the Eldorado and pulled the doors shut. Marshall started it up, and they pulled out of the lot and got back on the road.

"We're really low on gas," Marshall said. "I hope we find another town soon."

They listened to various reports on the radio, but no one seemed to have anything new to say. It was all just a rehash of what they already knew.

"What if it really is the apocalypse?" asked Wilson.

Cleavon said, "Nothing feels any different. I doubt it's the apocalypse. It seems like that would be a big enough thing that you'd know something was happening."

"I guess," said Wilson.

"Can you believe they're actually saying those groups of people may be corpses?" Cleavon asked. "That's just crazy-talk. I don't even know what to make of that. How could that many people be seeing the same crazy thing at the same time?"

"Mass hysteria?" asked Wilson.

"Maybe."

Marshall looked at him. "I wonder how they're killing people."

"What do you mean?" Cleavon asked.

"Those groups of crazy people or corpses or whatever they are," Marshall said. "They didn't say exactly how they were killing people. I mean, are they using guns? Knives? Are they beating people to death?"

"That's a good question," said Wilson. "I hadn't even thought about that."

"The question is, if you were a corpse, how would you kill people?" asked Marshall.

"This is ludicrous," Cleavon said. "Do you guys hear what you're saying?"

"It may be nonsense, but it's what they're saying on every single radio station," said Marshall. "How do *you* explain it?"

"I don't know," said Cleavon. "I'd have to see those mobs of crazy people first to assess what in the hell it is we're actually talking about. But I don't at this moment have it in me to believe without seeing them that they are actually dead people come back to life."

Marshall nodded. "I guess so."

"Besides, dead people *couldn't* come back to life," Cleavon said.

"Why is that?"

"They take out their blood and fill them with embalming fluid when they die," Cleavon said. "I don't think it would be possible for anything to live with a body filled with embalming fluid."

"Hmmm," said Marshall. "That's interesting."

"Is there any music on at all on that radio?" Cleavon asked.

Marshall turned through the channels, but found nothing.

"Sorry," said Marshall. "No music. Just more dead-people talk."

"I miss Sam and Dave already," said Wilson. "We were having a good time there for a minute."

"Yeah, those were better times," Cleavon said. "And that was only, what, an hour ago? And now we're talking about... I don't even know what we're talking about."

Wilson said, "Madness."

"No shit," said Cleavon. "This is just crazy."

"Indeed," said Marshall.

"If there are dead people out there," Wilson said, "what do you think brought them back to life?"

Cleavon said, "Damned if I know."

They drove for an hour, but did not come to another town.

Soon the car started sputtering and shook for a moment, running out of gas. Marshall maneuvered the dying Eldorado off the road.

"Fuck," said Marshall.

"Now what?" asked Wilson.

"We've gotta walk to find gas," Marshall said.

Wilson frowned. "Walk where?"

"How the fuck do I know?" Marshall said. "I've never been here before."

"You don't have a map?" asked Cleavon.

"Sadly, no," said Marshall.

"Good planning," said Wilson.

"I don't see you with a map either," Marshall said.

The three friends climbed out of the Eldorado.

"You got a gas can?" asked Cleavon.

Marshall shook his head. "No."

"What will we use for the gas?" asked Wilson.

"We'll have to improvise," Marshall said. "We'll figure it out when the time comes."

Marshall locked the car doors, and the three friends started to walk down the road. They walked for what felt like an hour or so, but did not see any houses or towns.

"Taking back roads kind of seems like a bad idea now, in retrospect," said Cleavon.

"Hindsight is 20/20," said Marshall.

They continued to walk until they came to a cemetery on the right side of the road. It was a large, lavish cemetery, unlike anything they had ever seen. As they approached it, Cleavon said, "I don't like being near a cemetery while they're talking about corpses attacking people."

"I thought you didn't believe that," said Wilson.

"I don't," Cleavon said. "But I don't wanna take any chances either."

"There aren't any dead people walking around over there," observed Marshall.

"Maybe they were just cadavers from universities that got loose," Wilson said. "I mean, how could dead people get out of the ground if they were alive?"

Cleavon nodded. "True."

The three friends walked towards the cemetery to see what exactly it was, why it was so lavish.

"This is a strange place," said Wilson.

"It is," said Marshall. "I've never seen anything like it."

There were huge statues of men riding on horses with swords, and hundreds of tiny Confederate flags adorned the graves.

"Is it a Civil War cemetery?" asked Cleavon.

"No," said Wilson, now understanding what this place was. "It's a Klu Klux Klan cemetery."

"It's a *what*?" asked Marshall.

"You heard me."

They saw a huge marble sign in front of the cemetery that read: THE NATHANIEL BEDFORD FORREST MEMORIAL CEMETERY FOR FALLEN SONS OF THE SOUTH.

"I didn't even know there was such a thing," said Marshall.

"Neither did I," Wilson said.

"Weird that it's out here in the middle of nowhere, on some back road," said Cleavon. "Really strange place for such a fancy cemetery."

"Well," said Wilson, "this may not have been a back road back when this cemetery was established. This may have been a fairly-busy road back then, before the highways came in."

Cleavon nodded. "Makes sense."

"Should we check it out?" asked Wilson.

"I vote no," said Marshall. "We need to find gas, and it'll be dark soon. Besides, I don't want to run into the crackers who maintain this place. Do you? Something tells me they aren't partial to Negroes lurking around here."

"A few minutes won't hurt anything," said Cleavon. "Besides, I've gotta take a leak."

Marshall and Wilson looked at each other as Cleavon approached the cemetery gates. Wilson shrugged.

"Maybe you ought to just piss out here by the road," Marshall said. "That way we don't have to worry about any racist rednecks showing up and getting mad because you're desecrating Uncle Wilbur's resting place."

Wilson chuckled.

Cleavon kept walking. The gate was unlocked. He unlatched it, and walked into the cemetery. He looked around, eyeballing the huge statues of Klansmen riding with their sabers raised. He also looked around at the lavish mausoleums.

"They really keep this place well-maintained," said Cleavon.

"Yeah," Wilson said, entering the cemetery gates. "This place is nicer than our school. This is nuts."

Cleavon found a grave with an engraving on its headstone of a Klansman being carried to heaven by an angel.

"Looks like as good a place as any," he said, unzipping his pants.

He let his penis hang out and started urinating on the headstone, turning to spray the little Confederate flag next to it, as well.

"Uncle Wilbur's gonna be pissed," Cleavon said, laughing.

Marshall was nervous. He looked around in both directions, but saw no one coming. "Please hurry," he said. "I really wanna get out of here."

Wilson was examining a huge marble mausoleum with the name THORNTON inscribed over its doorway. Wilson jokingly knocked on the door. "Anybody home?" he asked. He opened the door to the mausoleum and went inside for a more thorough investigation.

Once he was inside, he saw that a tomb drawer on his left was open.

And it was empty.

Where the hell was the body?

Wilson turned back towards the door and came face-to-face with a living corpse, its arms reaching out for him. Its clothing was ripped apart, and it was mostly skeletal by this point. The corpse's eyeballs were long gone and there were gaping holes where they had once been. Pieces of dried, leathery skin hung from the corpse's exposed jowls.

"What the fuck?" said Wilson.

The corpse moved towards him. There was nowhere for Wilson to go.

He screamed, but the scream became a grotesque gurgling sound as the corpse ripped Wilson's head from his neck.

Outside, Marshall and Cleavon were alarmed.

"Wilson?" asked Cleavon.

There was no response.

Marshall said, "Dammit, Wilson, this is no time for jokes. We don't have time for this."

Still no response.

"I'll check on him," said Cleavon, moving towards the open mausoleum. He walked around the thing, entering its doorway, not believing what he was seeing. It was fairly dark in there, so Cleavon couldn't see clearly. There was some sort of grotesquely-disfigured man hunched over Wilson, who was lying on the floor. The man had his head down, obstructing Cleavon's view so he couldn't see what the hell was happening.

"Hey!" Cleavon said. "What the fuck are you doing?"

The man looked up and Cleavon got a clear view of what was happening. When the man raised his face to look at Cleavon, he ripped skin from Wilson's already-torn-apart throat. The bloody meat was dangling from the man's mouth, blood dripping all over Wilson's dead body.

The man faced Cleavon, making a sort of grunting sound as he did.

Cleavon screamed.

He turned to run, took about two steps out of the mausoleum, and was immediately confronted by another of the rotten monstrosities, dressed in a tattered robe that had once been white. Cleavon stared at the thing for a second, realizing it was indeed a rotting corpse. He maneuvered around it.

The thing moved slowly, shambling towards him. Cleavon ran for Marshall, but found that his friend was in trouble, as well. In his peripheral vision, Cleavon could see dozens of figures moving around the cemetery now, but he paid them no mind. His focus was on Marshall, who was lying on the ground, wrestling with another of the dead men.

"Hey, asshole!" Cleavon said, trying to get the dead man's attention. The corpse turned to face him, appearing to look at him even though he had no eyeballs. Marshall, still lying under the thing, reached down to the corpse's side and unsheathed its saber, pushing it up through its crumbling body. The corpse raised up a bit, more frenzied than before, and tried to bite his face.

Cleavon attempted to distract the corpse again. "Hey, asshole!"

The dead man turned towards Cleavon, and Marshall repositioned the saber and brought it up hard through its eye socket. The thing made a dry, growling sound, and fell dead once again. Marshall pushed it off him, and started to get up. Cleavon came forward to assist him, but Marshall saw another dead man behind Cleavon.

"Cleavon!" he screamed. "Behind you!"

Cleavon whirled around and saw the dead man in the white robe. He pulled back his fist out of sheer instinct and punched its chest as hard as he could, his fist going clear through the corpse's body. This had no effect on the creature, and it moved closer towards him. Cleavon pulled his fist out of the dead man's chest, and kicked it hard in the knee. The dead man's leg gave in, crumbling upon contact, and the dead Klansman collapsed. Cleavon moved forward, raised his leg, and stomped hard, crushing the dead man's head. The corpse stopped moving.

Cleavon turned to face Marshall, now standing beside him.

"You believe in walking dead men now?" asked Marshall.

"I know how they kill people," Cleavon said, his voice wavering.

"How?"

"They eat you."

Marshall grimaced, a chill running down his spine.

The two friends suddenly realized they were slowly being surrounded by the slow-moving dead men. There were about ten of them in close proximity, and dozens more behind. It was getting dark now, and they could see the silhouettes of more figures off in the distance, some of them still crawling out of the ground.

"Coming here was a bad idea," said Cleavon.

Marshall looked at him. "I told you, but you don't listen."

Cleavon reached down over the dead man he'd just stopped and unsheathed its saber. The two men turned towards the horde, their backs to one another, sabers of dead Klansmen before them.

"You ready?" asked Cleavon.

"Shit no."

The dead men were closing in.

Cleavon struck first, lopping off the head of a corpse. Within seconds both of them were bobbing and weaving with their sabers, chopping off heads right and left. Both of them were winded with still more surrounding dead men left to battle. Cleavon buried his saber in the cheekbone of a dead man, pushing it through to the hilt. Soon the two men were standing there, back to back, exhausted, with a pile of decapitated Klansmen at their feet.

"Let's get out of here," said Marshall.

"Where do we go?"

"Anywhere but here."

The two of them slowly made their way through the cemetery, fighting off attacking dead men as they walked, chopping off rotten heads and arms at every turn. Finally they made their way back to the gate. They opened it and slipped out, quickly fastening it behind them. A crowd of the dead men was soon assembled there, trying to get out, but unable to comprehend the gate's latch.

"We did it," Marshall said.

Cleavon raised his hand and Marshall slapped him a five.

The two exhausted men then shuffled down the dirt road, looking like dead men themselves.

"The chances of us making it out of this are pretty slim," said Marshall.

Cleavon rolled his eyes. "You always know just what to say to ruin the mood."

"At least we got swords."

Cleavon chuckled. "Two century-old swords against thousands of walking dead men who want to eat us. What could possibly go wrong?"

FUBAR

First Sgt. Tommy McDougal had been home from Vietnam for three years now, but sometimes the horrors of war felt as close as they ever had. At night he dreamed of firefights and the sweltering heat of the jungle and attending to dead comrades, making him afraid to go to sleep. Sometimes he got lost in daydreams in which he was still out there in the bush, tracking down the Vietcong and killing them violently. He would be sitting in the living room and hear a sound, and reach for his absent M-16 out of habit.

Sgt. Tommy McDougal had left Vietnam, but the 'Nam refused to leave him.

He had hated every minute he'd spent in that godforsaken jungle, and yet he now found he could no longer relate to civilian life stateside. As much as he had hated the experience of war, he now found himself yearning for canteens and entrenching tools and semi-automatic weapons. He longed for the brotherhood he'd experienced amongst his platoon, and he wanted nothing more than to shoot a gook or two. Not because he was sadistic, and not because he enjoyed killing, but because he missed the familiarity the war had provided him with. In Vietnam, Tommy had a purpose. He was somebody, part of a unit. Here he was nobody.

Now he was lost. He'd come home to a country that didn't want him and didn't respect or understand the sacrifices he'd made. They'd spit on him and called him a baby-killer. They called him a monster. And maybe they were right. He had seen and done things in the bush that he wasn't proud of—things he would never speak of as long as he lived—and those actions were the stuff of his nightmares.

He was now living in a first-floor apartment in Queens, but he didn't dare leave the place if he could help it. When he attempted to go outside, he felt closed-in and panicked; he couldn't breathe; simply putting one foot in front of the other became an impossible task.

He had held a job as a security guard at Monkey Wards for a while, but then he'd suffered his debilitating mental breakdown and wound up living on his Uncle Sam's dime as yet another disabled vet.

He took the pills they had given him at the VA hospital, downing them with a swig of whiskey. He tried to watch television, but found himself unable to focus on anything other than sporting events and the news. In the daytime he found himself bombarded by what felt like a hundred pointless soap operas. He had nowhere to go to get away, but he didn't dare turn off the TV because he hated the silence almost as much as he hated himself. So he drank. A lot. And the TV blared on.

It was Friday, May the 13th when Tommy opened his eyes and realized he was back in 'Nam. He wasn't exactly sure where he was—he was trapped inside some type of structure, most likely behind enemy lines—but he knew enough to know it was Vietnam. He could smell it in his nostrils and taste it in his mouth. There was no place else like Vietnam, and Tommy thanked god for that.

He crawled to the window, pushing himself up to peer out at the world outside. Queens now became Hanoi. He saw people everywhere, making their way up and down the street, and knew at once they were enemy combatants. He made his way, still crawling, through the apartment, in search of his comrades, but he did not find them. His heart was in his throat, his pulse in his ears. He was alone here.

The situation was FUBAR—fucked up beyond all recognition. Here he was, unable to remember how he'd gotten into Hanoi, trapped inside this structure, behind enemy lines. He was surely a dead man. From here on, every move he made would have to be exactly the right one. There was no room for fuck ups; one slip-up, and he would be a goner.

Tommy crawled to the closet in the living room, somehow knowing there were weapons inside. He reached in and grabbed the two guns, and his rifles became enemy AK-47s. They were, of course, already loaded. He didn't like using the enemy rifles as they felt foreign in his hands, but he was glad to be armed. Who the hell knew what was lurking out there beyond that door?

Fuck! he thought. He'd really gotten himself into some deep shit here, and there was no one who could save him. The truth was Tommy had always felt he'd relied a little too much on his fellow soldiers; he did his job, but he had always been afraid to go above and beyond the call of duty for fear of death. He'd been cowardly, although no one had ever known or made note of it. But here would be his chance for redemption. This would be his own private war—one that wasn't about guts and glory but survival.

Tommy crawled back over to the window and pushed himself up into a squatting position. He looked out at the street and watched the unsuspecting VC moving around out there. They had no idea he was here, an unwanted guest, tucked away within their little sanctuary. These gooks walked to and fro, up and down the street, without so much as a thought to the possibility of being observed by a U.S. soldier. At least he would have the element of surprise on his side. He would just have to wait until something or someone forced his hand, because once he fired that first shot, there was no turning back.

He now wondered how much food there was inside this hovel. He crawled into the kitchen, somehow knowing just where to locate it. He stood carefully, looking around as he did, and then opened the cabinet door, scanning the cans inside. There were enough C-rations there to last him a week. There were cans of pork and beans, cream corn, and mixed vegetables. There were even a couple of cans of Spam to tide him over. *Good,* he thought. *American food. None of that curry bullshit.* Tommy closed the cabinet door and scanned the kitchen in search of further subsistence. Then he saw the bottle of sour mash whiskey sitting there on the cabinet, and he started to feel at ease.

Well, he thought, *at least I'll have old Jack Daniels to keep me company while I'm trapped inside this rat-trap.* He twisted the lid off the bottle and took a drink, the warm liquid sliding down his throat easily, warming his chest and belly as it went. He then crawled back to the spot where the rifles were, beside the window. He rooted himself there and went to work on the bottle of whiskey.

And he waited.

And waited.

Day turned to night and night turned to day.

Without a radio to call in for assistance, he had no choice but to wait for a sign. So he sat and preoccupied himself with thoughts of the Vietnam he remembered. He wondered how he'd gotten here, and why he could no longer remember it. Was this his third tour of the 'Nam, or was it still his second? He now wondered if maybe civilian life had been the dream—an awful nightmare from which he'd finally broken free—and this was his true reality. He tried to concentrate, tried to remember anything that could inform him as to his purpose here, but he found that he could not pull up a single clue.

Finally, after what felt like an eternity of waiting, there was a knock at the door. Did they know he was here? Or even better, could it be his comrades here to save him? He couldn't be sure without opening the door. He stood up, moving towards the apartment door, letter opener in hand. He moved stealthily, and there came a second knock. Tommy quietly unlocked the chain and opened the door.

There was a man standing there, the fat delivery guy from the party store down the street. Tommy saw him every other day, three to four times a week. But he didn't recognize him now. Today Tommy saw Victor Charlie standing there, and the sack of alcohol the man carried now became a pistol. Tommy moved instinctively, pulling away the enemy combatant's gun, and burying his blade in his throat, blood spraying all around. He held Charlie close, his hand over his mouth, and waited for him to stop convulsing. Once Charlie was dead, Tommy pulled him into the apartment and flung him into the corner like an unwanted rag doll. He shut the door behind him, hoping he hadn't been heard.

Tommy's head was spinning. He'd drawn first blood, and now it was only a matter of time before Charlie's friends came looking for him. He had to make his move. Now was the moment he had to take action.

Tommy grabbed the rifles, carrying one and slinging the other across his back. He went back to the door, opened it, and peeked around in both directions, making sure the corridor outside was clear. He moved quickly now, a professional soldier in action. He made his way down the hall to a glass door on his left. When he got there, he looked outside and saw a Puerto Rican guy riding a lawn mower, trimming the grass surrounding the apartment building.

Tommy had never seen a militarized vehicle such as this one, but knew he must commandeer it now if he wanted to survive. He waited until the PR took the corner and turned around, and he sprung through the door. He rushed up behind the man, pulling him off the back of the mower and burying his blade in his throat. He then climbed on top of the riding mower, stomped on the gas, and steered it towards the busy street. When he reached it, the mower made a loud scraping sound as it jumped the curb.

Tommy was now aware that the pedestrians were staring at him, watching his every movement attentively. He drove the mower up close to an old man walking his dog—definitely a Vietcong soldier—and lowered his rifle. He squeezed the trigger and shot the old man in the chest, sending him reeling back against the pavement.

He looked down the street and saw that there were people and automobiles everywhere. There was no way he could possibly make it out of here alive. He would just have to go out shooting and hope for the best.

COMMUNION SUNDAY

Fresh off a painful break-up with her married boss, Phillip, Kat badly needed a vacation. She hadn't taken one in years and, frankly, had no idea where she would go, but figured anywhere outside St. Louis sounded great. Her sister, Theresa, wanted her to visit her family in Nowheresville, Kansas. Kat had never wanted to go to such a place, had long avoided visiting her sister's dreadful little family, and believed rural Kansas sounded a lot like hell on Earth. But now, for the first time ever, she found herself actually considering such a trip. After all, it was within driving distance and she wouldn't know anyone outside of Theresa and her stupid family. Kat didn't need to go anywhere fancy—she just needed to get *away*.

So here she was at work, sitting in her cubicle, finishing a Sudoku puzzle and talking to her sister on the phone. It was ten till five and she was just killing time now, waiting for five o'clock to roll around so she could get the hell out of there.

"You really should consider coming to Upton next week," Theresa said. "I think you'd like it here. And if you come next week, you'll be here for Communion Sunday."

Much to Kat's chagrin, her beloved baby sis Theresa had become a bonafide Bible-thumper. Kat herself wasn't so much of an atheist as she simply didn't give a shit one way or the other. But Theresa, she was a different story. She talked about God and Jesus and the people at her church and Minister Dave, her preacher, all the damned time. Any conversation with Theresa was sure to find its way to conservative politics and religion. She loved God and hated Obama; Jesus was swell and Bill Maher was the anti-Christ. And you didn't want to get her started on those brown-skinned illegal aliens... Or those pesky gays...

Oh, yes, rural Kansas. They were so enlightened there. Kat couldn't wait to visit.

"What's so special about Communion Sunday?" Kat asked.

"Well," Theresa said, "at a lot of churches they have communion every week, but at our church, the First Faith Church of Upton, we only have communion once a month. It's a very special time—the most special time in our faith—when we can show God our thanks for all the things we're happy about. It's a time to meet new church visitors. It's a special time of worship and love."

Puke, thought Kat.

"What else do you do in Upton besides go to church?" Kat asked.

There was a pause at the other end of the line and Kat could tell the question had offended her now easily-offended baby sis. "Well, you know, we have a movie theater," Theresa said. "They only show wholesome PG and G-rated family films. It isn't like up there in St. Louis, where the temptations of the devil are all around. Here we keep it simple...and wholesome...just the way God intended."

Double puke, thought Kat.

"So you gonna come down and see us?" asked Theresa.

"I'm not sure."

"Oh, come on, sis. You *have* to come. You just have to."

"Oh, I do, do I? Why is that?"

"Because we haven't seen each other in ages. How long's it been now? Three years? Four?"

Kat pretended not to know, knowing damn well it had been five years since they'd seen one another. But that was back when Theresa was a normal person—before she'd become singularly obsessed with God. That was before she started quoting the likes of Rush Limbaugh, Jesus, and Donald Rumsfeld. That was when the two sisters could have a normal conversation about things from the real world without either of them walking away confused or hurt.

But what the hell? It had been five years, and Kat really needed to get away. She needed to go somewhere, *anywhere*, that wasn't St. Louis. She needed a break from her life, her job, and most of all Phillip.

"Sure, I'll come," Kat said.

"Next week?"

Kat sighed. "Sure. Next week."

"Good. You can sleep in Tabby's room."

"No, no, don't trouble yourself."

"Oh, it's no bother for a VIP like yourself."

"Really," Kat said. "Don't bother. The truth is I'd rather stay in a motel. Are there any motels there?"

"Oh, sure," Theresa said, trying to sound upbeat despite being hurt that her sister didn't want to stay with her. "There's a real nice motel out on the highway. It's pretty new."

"How new?"

"Well, I'm sure it's been built since the last time I saw you."

Kat smiled at that little passive aggressive jab. "Okay," she said. "I'll make reservations just as soon as I get off the phone."

And then the conversation continued on to Kat's hedonistic lifestyle, the power of Almighty God, and how gay people were destroying family values in America. None of this made Kat any more excited about visiting her sister's family in Crapville, Kansas, but she kept her mouth shut and listened to her sister rant.

The following Saturday, Kat embarked upon the five hour drive to Upton, Kansas, home of the undefeated Upton Gators high school football team, lots of red-blooded redneck white 'Mericans, and everyone's favorite day, Communion Sunday. Kat loaded up the little Honda with enough clothes to last a month (even though she was only staying for a week), and climbed in behind the steering wheel. She snapped her seat belt and opened her CD case, searching for just the right thing to listen to on this epic drive to nowhere. She finally settled on The Beatles' *Rubber Soul* album, skipped to track eleven, "In My Life," and pulled out of her apartment parking lot.

She dug around in her purse while driving, fished out a nice, fat joint, and raised it to her lips. She let it dangle there for a moment, lighting it with her Aerosmith Zippo. She took a nice drag off the joint, held the smoke in her chest for a moment, and then let it float out from her nostrils. She started to sing along with The Beatles, quickly got bored, and skipped to track seven, the perennial favorite "Michelle." She sang along, even attempting to repeat the French words she didn't know, knowing she would replay this song another dozen or so times before moving on to another song or CD.

Soon she was on the highway with St. Louis in her rearview mirror, feeling high and alive in a way she hadn't felt in a good long time. She sang "Michelle" over and over again, and before long a couple hours had passed. She pulled over at some little nondescript town, parked in the driveway of Mickey D's, and went inside and had a Big Mac, an order of large fries with way too much salt, and a chocolate shake to cover up the taste of the meal, which was so-so even by McDonalds standards.

Soon she was back on the road, pushing the little Honda up past ninety, smoking another joint, and singing along to Billy Joel's "Big Shot." She was feeling good; so good, in fact, she doubted even the reality of Shit Stain, Kansas would be able to spoil her mood.

After a full four joints, three Valium, and a couple wrong turns, Kat eventually found her way to Upton, and it was all she imagined it would be. When she first approached the city limits, she saw a huge sign which read "God and Guns—Keep America Safe!" This sign was surrounded by several miles of anti-abortion billboards, which said things like "Choose Life—Your Mother Did!" and the always-creative "Abortion Is Murder!" Seeing these signs didn't exactly make Kat feel bad about her own abortion. It was akin to seeing an anti-smoking ad and then craving a cigarette. It wasn't that she craved to have another abortion—she had already had two in her thirty-two years of life—so much as it made her reflect on the action matter-of-factly the way a McDonalds ad would have caused her to reflect upon lunch.

Once she got to the Upton City Limits, Pop. 1,212, she saw another sign boasting that the "city" was the birthplace of famous professional wrestler Rufus "Red" Managold. Kat was used to St. Louis, which was the home of multiple professional sports teams, poet Maya Angelou, and lots of other really cool people. And here was this itty-bitty shithole bragging about some stupid wrassler.

Kat found Upton to be a lot like being trapped inside an episode of *Duck Dynasty*; everyone looked stupid, wore camouflage clothes, and donned Jesus-related T-shirts with quirky little slogans on them.

She checked into her motel, a generic, overly-sanitized place appropriately dubbed Sleep-In Motel. *Who the hell came up with that name?* Kat wondered. Whoever it was, they couldn't have been particularly proud of that one.

Kat paid for five days.

"What are the hours for the pool?" she asked, dying for a swim.

The guy behind the counter, Ernest, said, "Oh, the pool's closed."

Kat could have killed him. "Why?"

"Someone went to the bathroom in it and it had to be cleaned."

"All that because someone peed in it?"

"No," the man said, visibly embarrassed. "They took a Number Two."

"Ah," said Kat. "When do you anticipate it being open again?"

"Not for another week or so."

Goddammit, Kat thought. *All I wanted was to go for a swim.*

"Is there another motel around here?" she asked. "One with a pool?"

"Oh, yeah," Ernest said, staring off into the distance, as if he could see through the wall. "There's a real nice one in Kincaid."

"How far away is Kincaid?"

"About an hour."

And that was it—no pool for Kat.

"All right, thanks," she said.

As she started to walk out of the lobby, Ernest called to her, "Hey, lady."

She turned and looked at him. "Yeah?"

"Are you going to Communion Sunday?"

She forced a smile. "Wouldn't miss it for the world."

Kat telephoned Theresa to get directions to her house. When she got into her car, she noticed it was almost out of gas, so she pulled into the local filling station. To her surprise, there was still a gas station attendant working there. He came out and pumped her gas, cleaned the windows, and checked her oil.

"You new in town?" the man asked, looking up from the dipstick.

"I'm just staying for a few days."

"Ah, you got family around here?"

Kat nodded. "My sister and her family live here."

"Oh, that's nice," the man said, closing the hood.

He told her it would be twenty-five dollars. She paid him in cash and started to climb back into the car. Before she could get in, he asked, "You gonna be here for Communion Sunday?"

Kat grinned. "That's a pretty big day around here, huh?"

"Oh, the biggest," the man said.

"Yeah, I'll definitely be there."

She started the car and the sound of Steven Tyler singing "Sweet Emotion" came blaring out the window. The gas station attendant, unsure what to think about all this, just watched her pull out of the parking lot.

"Crazy goddamn city folk," he said, shaking his head.

Dinner with Theresa and her family—hubby Frank, daughter number one Emily, daughter number two Amy, and son Noah—was painful as hell. The meal consisted of a KFC bucket of chicken with sides of cole slaw and mashed potatoes with gravy. The mostly-one-sided conversation consisted of a lot of God, the devil, and Glenn Beck talk. Finally, when she felt she could take no more, Kat tried to bow out.

"What's wrong?" Theresa asked. "It's still early. We could still play a game or two of Bible Trivial Pursuit."

"No," Kat said. "I'm not feeling well."

"I hope it wasn't the chicken."

"I don't think it was," Kat said. "I wasn't feeling great before that."

"Well, you need to go back to your room and get some rest anyway," Theresa said. "After all, tomorrow morning's Communion Sunday. You need to be rested up so you're feeling well for that."

"How could I forget?" Kat asked.

"Trust me, you won't want to forget that. It's a very special day."

Kat excused herself, went back to her room, smoked a joint, drank a fifth of scotch, and watched a pay-per-view movie called *Lesbians Like It Wet*. She set the alarm on her phone—god knows she wouldn't want to miss out on the much-ballyhooed Communion Sunday—and went to bed, falling fast asleep.

The next morning Kat met Theresa and Frank and all their rugrats at their house. Theresa and Frank were color-coordinated, and the kids all wore Jesus T-shirts and cargo shorts.

"Are you ready to experience God in a way you never have before?" Theresa asked enthusiastically.

Kat said, "Sure."

"Our church is very special. It's one of a kind. We've got a band, and nobody can give a sermon like Minister Dave can. He's amazing. It's as if God really speaks through him...like he's a vessel of the Lord. You know, several churches—several *big* churches—were in competition for Minister Dave when he needed a job. He could have gone anywhere he wanted, but he came here."

"Why?" Kat asked.

Theresa looked at Frank as if she couldn't believe Kat would ask such a thing. "Why, he came here because God told him to. Don't you know that, Kat? We *all* go where God leads us. Even you."

Kat laughed, thinking her sister was an imbecile, but said nothing.

The First Faith Church of Upton was a rundown little shithole, the kind of bland little hovel that doubled as Alcoholics Anonymous during the week. The people inside the building were clearly at odds with the building itself. The people were as annoyingly upbeat and cheerful as anyone Kat had ever experienced. A lot of them were dressed nicely, just as Kat had seen in church as a child, but most of them were wearing T-shirts that said things like GOD'S GYM and GOD IS NOT DEAD.

Minister Dave was the worst of all. He had spiky hair, jumped around as if he was tweaking on meth, and reminded Kat of Vince, the ShamWow TV spokesman who had gotten into trouble a few years back for beating up a hooker. Kat hated this fucking guy, and she wanted nothing more than to punch him in his big, dumb, smarmy, smiling face.

"I think you're gonna like it here," Minister Dave said. "I can just feel it. In fact, I *know* it. God told me." And he gave her a creepy wink, sending a chill down her spine.

The first thirty minutes of the service was just your normal, run-of-the-mill church service, complete with a sermon about how the Earth was only 6,000 years old and how men and dinosaurs once coexisted. After that, things started to get weird.

"I need all the first-time visitors to come up front," Minister Dave said.

Kat looked at Theresa, not wanting to go, but her sister held up her hand and pointed down, illuminating her.

Minister Dave stepped down from behind the podium. "Come on up, sister," he told Kat. "I want all you newbies—that's what I call first-timers—to come on up here so we can praise God together!"

Kat was now standing in the aisle, and an elderly man with a yellowed mullet came to escort her up to the front of the church. She looked around and saw a few other people being led to the front. Most of them were smiling widely, but a couple of them, like her, were visibly nervous.

Before Kat reached the front, she saw Minister Dave lift an oblong oak box from behind the podium. On the box it said "DO THIS IN REMEMBRANCE OF ME." Minister Dave stepped down towards the first newcomer.

"How are you, my good man?" Minister Dave asked.

The man said he was good, and Minister Dave opened the box, removing a shotgun from inside. He sat down the box and raised the shotgun, leveling it at the man's face.

"What the hell?" the man managed.

Minister Dave squeezed the trigger.

BLAM!

The man's head exploded into a gooey mess of blood, brains, and skull. Minister Dave looked to the next woman, who was being held in place by a couple of old men. Terrified, Kat turned and ran towards the doors, but throngs of churchgoers crowded in front of her, blocking her exit. She could feel them clawing at her, pulling her hair, and she heard Minister Dave's voice growing closer to her.

"John 6:54," he was saying loudly. "He whomever eats of the flesh and drinks of the blood shall have everlasting life!"

That was when Kat felt the first bite being taken out of her arm.

SACRIFICIAL CATS

The newest story was up on his website *Haunted Happenings*, and Mike Lanahan was feeling accomplished. The piece he'd just put up detailed his stay at the supposedly-haunted Crescent Hotel in Eureka Springs, Arkansas. He'd paid through the nose to stay at the old hotel, and had really, really hoped to come face to face with a supernatural entity. But he didn't. He never did. Even the old Ouija board he'd brought had failed to summon any sort of supernatural beings.

Instead of documenting any supernatural activity, Mike had spent most of his night at the Crescent arguing with his mistress, Natalie. This was how most of his trips went these days. Natalie would insist upon going (Mike naturally left this detail out of his accounts on the website), and she would then wind up growing irritated and wanting to argue with him.

And their spats weren't interesting in the least.

They were always the same.

Always.

Without exception.

"Why don't you leave your wife so we can be together?" she would say.

And Mike really wanted to leave Beth, and he could sometimes see a real future for himself with Natalie, but their arguments only pushed him further away from pulling the trigger on such a thing. He loved Natalie, truly he did, but she had grown quite difficult as of late. It wasn't like five years ago, back when she was always fun and bubbly—back when she still believed his lies.

He knew five years was a long time to string a beautiful young woman along, but he wanted to be one-hundred-percent certain when he made the decision to break up his marriage. What Natalie refused to see was that absolutely none of Mike's reasoning to stay with Beth over the years had had anything in the least to do with Beth herself. No, Beth was bland. Beth was boring. She had zero personality. She just did and thought whatever Mike did and thought. He liked to joke behind closed doors that Beth was tofu—that she had no distinctive flavor of her own, but merely took on the flavor of whatever was around her. It was a funny analogy, but it was also a truthful one. She had also grown fat, and Mike now found her unattractive.

So why had Mike stayed with Beth? She loved him, for one thing. And she had a really good job working as a consultant for an investment firm. And financial security was a very important thing. Mike couldn't see breaking things off with Beth just to get into a tumultuous relationship with a nag. Beth treated him like a king, which was more than he could say for Natalie. Sure, Natalie was hot, and sure, she was great in the sack, but sometimes those things just didn't seem like enough to build a life around.

Then there was another school of thought that said maybe Natalie would return to being her old, fun self and would be less bitchy once Mike actually gave her what she wanted. But that seemed like one hell of a gamble, and he just wasn't sure he could afford to take such a risk.

So things went on just as they always had.

Today, just after Mike had posted the Crescent Hotel story, he received a message on the site from a reader named Mark telling him about a place called Stull, Kansas, that was said to be the seventh gate to hell. "You should cover that place," the e-mail said. "I have always wanted to go there, but I live two states away. But if you're in Kansas City, then it's within driving range for you."

Somehow Mike had never heard about this place, and had never heard the legends of it being a gateway to hell. So he looked it up on the Internet, and immediately found hundreds of pages devoted to the tale. According to the Internet, Stull was hardly even a town—just a scattering of rundown little farmhouses. And a cemetery. The legend said the gateway to hell was inside the Stull cemetery, beneath an old boarded-up church that had supposedly been built over it. Apparently the cemetery was watched quite closely, and fences kept out gawkers and looky-loos. According to legend, back in the old days, people used to go into the cemetery at midnight and leave animal sacrifices for Lucifer and his demons. It was an interesting story. Bullshit, to be sure. But interesting bullshit never the less.

Some pages on the Internet claimed that when the Pope had flown over the United States, he had requested that the plane's route be altered so he wouldn't have to fly over Stull.

Mike knew he would have to go and check this place out. It had ample pedigree to warrant an investigation, and it was only a couple hours away from where Mike lived. This was a can't-miss proposition to be sure.

Mike called up his buddy, Ron. "There's this place called Stull, Kansas, and there's supposed to be a gateway to hell there," he said. "People used to go out there at midnight and leave sacrifices for Lucifer on the steps of this creepy old church."

"Do you believe in any of it?" asked Ron.

"Fuck no."

"So what's up?"

"I wondered if you wanted to go down there with me and help me check it out."

Ron thought about it for a moment. "Will we get arrested?"

"I sure hope not."

Ron's voice lightened. "That's not very reassuring."

"Sorry. It's all I got."

"Why aren't you taking Natalie?"

"I could kind of use a break from her," Mike said. "Besides, this isn't a stay-over. It should just take a few hours."

"At midnight?"

"Right, at midnight."

"You're gonna offer up an animal sacrifice?"

"Yeah, I figured I would."

"You should offer up Beth as your sacrifice," Ron said. "That would solve all your problems."

Mike laughed. "She's too big."

"What do you mean?"

"She's too much woman for Lucifer to handle."

They both laughed at this.

"Poor Beth," said Ron.

Mike said, "Poor Beth? *Poor Lucifer!*"

They both chuckled again.

"So what are you gonna use for your sacrifice?"

"Natalie has those two cats that someone dumped over at her place," Mike said. "She hasn't even named the little fuckers yet. I figure I'll take one of those poor bastards out there and offer it up on the steps of that church. If demons eat him, then good, and if not, I'll just leave him out there."

"Good plan. So when do you wanna go?"

"You doing anything tomorrow?"

"Tomorrow? I was thinking of watching *Alien 3* again, since I'm re-watching the first two tonight."

"Ugh."

"Nothing I can't put off for a day or two. *Alien 3* will still be there."

"So, are we on?"

"Yes, sir," said Ron.

And the plan was set.

The next night, Mike had one of the little gray tabby cats tied closed inside a pillowcase so he wouldn't get away. The pillowcase, which occasionally jumped around a bit, sat in the backseat of the car. Mike was driving, and Ron was in the passenger seat, fucking around with the stereo.

Mike's cell phone rang. It was Natalie.

He picked up. "Hello?"

"Hey, did you take one of the cats?"

"I did."

"Why?"

"It's a long story."

Natalie sat on the other end of the phone for a minute, thinking. "Are you going out there to that devil place...that gate to hell...*without me?*"

Mike and Ron exchanged glances.

"I am," he said.

"Why didn't you take me?"

"I wanted to check it out first," Mike said. "I didn't want you to get hurt."

"You don't actually believe there's a gateway to hell out there, do you?"

"No, baby," said Mike, "but I didn't want to take any chances. Not with you."

But his ploy didn't work, and Natalie bitched at him for the next thirty minutes.

Finally he managed to get off the phone just before they reached the metropolis that was Stull, Kansas. First they did a drive-by, looking around to see where everything was. Then, satisfied that no one was out, they turned around and hooked a right down the old road leading to Stull Cemetery.

Ron had "Highway to Hell" playing on the stereo, and they both laughed.

But Mike felt a little bit uneasy.

He wasn't sure why.

Maybe it was the dark, moonless night. Maybe it was the chilly night air.

Maybe it was Stull fucking Cemetery.

Once they arrived at the cemetery, they idled the car up to the side of the road, and turned out the headlights. No need to announce their arrival. Mike just wanted to get in, and get back out without anyone being the wiser.

Mike and Ron climbed out of the car. Ron went around to the back hatch and grabbed the flashlight. Mike snatched up the pillowcase containing the angry cat.

There was a big chain-link fence surrounding the old wrought-iron fence of the cemetery. Ron climbed over the fence first. He momentarily snagged his shirt on the top of the fence, but managed to wriggle free without too much effort. Mike then tossed the pillowcase containing the cat over the fence to Ron, who caught it like an all-star wide-receiver. The cat made an angry mewing sound from inside the bag, but neither man paid it any mind.

Now Mike climbed over the fence. His climb went as smoothly as one could have hoped for. Once he was back down on the ground, he checked his watch. "We only have about ten minutes."

The two men made their way over the second fence. They then walked through the dark, creepy old cemetery towards the ancient white church in the center of the grounds.

"This place is pretty fucking creepy," said Ron.

Mike agreed. "Yeah, it actually is pretty damned creepy."

"Now what?"

"Well," Mike said in a hushed whisper, "we sit the pillowcase down on the steps of the church, and we turn around."

"Turn around?"

"Yeah, the legend says you can't stare directly at the emerging demons or they'll take you with them."

"Then how will we know if they're there?"

"I dunno," said Mike.

He walked up to the old boarded-up church building, a chill running down his spine. He sat the wiggling pillowcase, still tied shut, down on the steps of the church.

"How far out do you think we need to walk away from the church?" asked Ron.

"I'm not sure."

And they started walking.

They got about twenty feet away from the church when they saw a bright light shining from behind them, their shadows stretched out far ahead. They heard a loud growling noise, and then what sounded like cackling.

The last sound they heard was the piercing scream of the cat.

And the light was gone.

Just like that.

Still turned away from the church, Ron looked at Mike incredulously. "You think it's safe to turn around?"

"Damned if I know."

"So what do we do?"

"I guess we wait another few minutes to make sure they're gone."

"Do you actually believe that just happened?" Ron asked.

Mike shook his head. "I'm not sure what the hell I believe."

They waited another ten minutes before turning around and looking back at the old church. It appeared to be normal, with nothing about it seeming out of place. They approached the steps where the pillowcase had been.

When they shined the flashlight on the steps, they could see dark red blood all over them.

And there was something else there.

Something small lying in the middle of the blood stain.

They walked closer to examine the object. When they got there, they were startled to find that it was the cat's leg, ripped apart from the rest of its body. There were no other pieces of the feline to be found. Just that one leg.

Mike looked at Ron, and then the two of them turned and ran as fast as they could.

In the car on the way home, Mike asked, "What the hell did we just see?"

Ron just looked at him, saying nothing.

"What do you think happened there?" Mike asked again.

"I think we both know what happened there. I don't fucking believe it, but it happened."

"Well, we didn't actually *see* it, so we can't say for sure what happened."

Ron shook his head. "Just keep telling yourself that lie."

They drove in silence for another couple of miles. Finally Mike spoke up and said, "Why don't we agree to never speak of this again, for as long as we both live?"

Ron said, "Deal."

And that was that.

But that wasn't that. Not as far as Natalie was concerned. She refused to let the conversation about what had happened in Stull die. She wanted details. First, she'd called repeatedly during Mike and Ron's trip back to KC. Neither of them wanted to revisit what they'd seen aloud, and Mike had just let the damn phone ring. He just didn't feel like talking with Natalie about the incident, and right then arguing seemed trite and ridiculous in the face of what they'd just encountered.

But when Mike had gotten back to Natalie's place, she'd harped on him and harped on him, hounding him about what he'd seen. Mike tried to lie about it, but she saw through it. Finally, he relented.

"So what did you see?" asked Natalie.

"There's something out there all right."

"What?"

"I can't say for sure, but something."

"What did you see?"

And Mike recounted for her the events which had transpired in Stull Cemetery, explaining what they had seen with their own eyes and what they had heard and experienced. He told her about the cat leg.

"I wanna see for myself," said Natalie.

Mike didn't want to go back.

"I want to go tomorrow night," she said.

"Tomorrow night?"

"What?"

"I'm really not in the mood to go back out there."

"What are you, some kind of pussy? Of course you are. You won't even leave your stupid wife for the woman you love."

And so on.

The next night, Mike made the familiar drive back to Stull. This time he was taking Natalie and Cat Number Two, once again tied up inside a pillowcase. The pillowcase jumped around a little, and the cat made a few unhappy noises from within it.

They were driving along the highway when Natalie started in again.

"So why won't you leave Beth?"

"I don't want to talk about this right now."

"You never want to talk about it."

"Not really, no."

"But we *need* to talk about it."

"Why?"

"Well," Natalie said, "I need to know if I'm wasting my time. I need to know if this relationship is ever gonna go anywhere."

"I just need to know the time is right before I leave her."

"When is the time ever gonna be any better? It hasn't been any better yet, and it's been five fucking years."

Mike tried to reassure her that everything was going to be okay.

But this time the conversation was different.

This time Natalie was talking about leaving.

"Why would you do that?" asked Mike.

"Why not? It's been five years."

"But it's been a good five years, hasn't it?"

"For you, yeah."

"What does that mean?"

Natalie laughed. "It means you've had your cake and you've gotten to eat it, too. You've had the nice life at home with wifey, and then you've had your piece on the side."

"Please don't leave me," Mike said.

"Why should I stay?"

"Things are gonna be different."

Natalie perked up.

Mike added, "I just need time."

Natalie rolled her eyes. "I think it's time for me to give up on this."

"On this?"

"On us."

He drove on, saying nothing.

Finally, after thirty minutes of uncomfortable silence, they arrived at the Stull Cemetery.

Mike walked around to the back hatch of the car, opened it, and pulled out some bungee cords.

"What are those for?" Natalie asked.

"All part of the process," Mike said.

Natalie looked into the back seat of the car. "Should I grab the cat?"

Mike smiled. "Yeah, we wouldn't wanna leave that guy behind."

They climbed the fence with no problems. It started to rain softly, lightning stretching out across the sky. Once they were inside the cemetery, Mike looked at his watch. He had fifteen minutes, and there was still a lot to do.

He looked at Natalie, who was looking the other direction.

Mike raised the flashlight and brought it down hard against the back of Natalie's head, knocking her unconscious. He then dragged her to the steps of the church, the rain in his eyes, and started tying her up with the bungee cords.

He was still tying her when she came to.

"What are you doing?" she asked frantically.

"I'm making a sacrifice to Lucifer."

"No," she cried. "Please don't."

"You're not gonna leave me," Mike said. "Not *ever*."

"I'm sorry. I won't go."

"I know you won't."

She started to speak again, but he gagged her with a piece of torn shirt.

He looked at his watch and saw that he had two minutes to get away from the church steps. He picked up the pillowcase containing Cat Number Two and started carrying it away from the building. He opened the pillowcase as he did, holding the cat, and stroking it as he walked.

A bright light came from behind him, once again throwing his shadow far out ahead.

He heard the loud growling sound, and this time it sounded like more than one person was laughing. Then he heard Natalie's muffled screams, and he realized he was smiling. It was then he realized he'd just unburdened himself of the albatross around his neck. Life was improving by the second.

He continued walking, stroking the cat. He looked out beyond the fence and now saw legions of faces standing there in the drizzle, watching him solemnly. They were the people of Stull. This frightened Mike, although he wasn't sure why.

He kept walking. As he did, he felt a light tap on his shoulder, startling him.

He turned around and saw the contorted black face of Lucifer there, his ram-like horns gnarled and disfigured. His eyes were deep and red and scary. His mouth was gaping open—huge, sharp fangs throughout—a sort of grin there, the smell of burnt death heavy on his breath.

"Going somewhere?" asked Lucifer.

"Oh, shit," Mike managed, dropping the cat.

First he felt himself lose control of his bladder.

Then he felt himself actually lose his bladder.

Lucifer whisked him off to hell, demons ripping him to shreds as he did.

And the residents of Stull turned away from the fence and returned to their homes.

THE MONSTER-KILLERS CLUB

Chad and his best friend David were both sitting Indian-style in Chad's living room, watching the latest episode of their favorite television show, *The Monster-Killers Club*. Chad and David were still young at nine-years-old, but both knew without a doubt that this episode, "Monsters in the Closet," was by far the best episode they'd ever seen. The scene where the two child monster killers started the Chupacabra's head on fire was epic, sure to be something they would discuss for weeks to come.

When the show was over, there was still a full hour of daylight left for them to go out into the backyard and recreate their favorite scenes from the show. One of the show's two monster killers was Sarah, a girl, so they could hardly pretend to be her. This left both boys wanting to be Ben. So they took turns being Ben and the Chupacabra.

"*Rowrrrr!*" growled Chupacabra David.

"I will defeat you, you filthy monster," said Chad as Ben, wielding a plastic sword. "I will cut your head off!"

"*Rowrrrr!*" repeated Chupacabra David.

And Chad was on him, pushing him down to the ground and spearing him repeatedly in the midsection with the sword. Chad raised the sword over his head, bringing it down hard, pretending to spear the Chupacabra once more. David, still in character, wiggled around violently for a matter of moments, dying a long, melodramatic death, the plastic sword protruding from his armpit. And then, finally, he stopped moving, and the Chupacabra was no more.

Chad reached down and grabbed David's hand, helping him up.

"Now let's trade places," David said.

"*Again?*" asked Chad. David sometimes found that Chad could be difficult to appease, and this was one such moment.

David rubbed his head. "Well, what do you wanna do?"

"I dunno," Chad said. "I wanna do something else."

"You wanna ride bikes?"

Chad thought it over for a minute, but shook his head. "Nah."

"We could trade comic books. I'll swap you the new *Batman* and the new *Spider-Man* for *Monster-Killers Club* number four."

Chad shook his head no. "That's my favorite."

"Well, then, what?" David asked.

"You wanna go to the park?" Chad lived directly across the street from the park, so there was no worry of them staying out too late.

"I dunno," David said, shrugging. "I guess."

So they went to the park, walking through the graveyard of empty park toys. The fall wind was cool, the empty swings blowing limply, and the dried brown leaves crunching under their feet. They talked about school and TV and the impending World Series as they walked. Then, finally, Chad said, "You know what I *really* wanna do?"

David did not.

"I wanna start our own Monster-Killers Club."

David wrinkled up his nose, unsure what his best friend was talking about. "What do you mean?"

"I mean a real-life Monster-Killers Club," Chad said. "You know, like Sarah and Ben on the TV show. We could hunt down real-life monsters and, you know, bring them to bloody justice."

David wasn't sure. "But..."

"But what?"

"Well, there aren't any monsters in Maybridge. It's not like in Chicago, where they live on the show, where there are monsters everywhere. I've never even seen even one monster in Maybridge—*ever.*"

Chad nodded. "I guess you're right. I don't think I've ever seen a single monster here, either."

"Why do you figure so many monsters live in Chicago?"

Chad thought about it for a moment. "Who knows? Monsters aren't like regular people. Who knows what goes through their heads?"

And at that, Chad's mother called for him to come home.

Chad and David gave each other the monster-killer handshake and went their separate ways.

Nine days passed, and not a day went by in which Chad and David didn't dream of being real-life versions of Sarah and Ben. The next week's episode, "Murder and Mayhem," had been a rerun, but it was one of the better episodes, and did little to end their desire to start their own version of the Monster-Killers Club.

It was a Wednesday night, and Chad's family was sitting down at the dinner table. Chad's mother and father were chattering enthusiastically about adult matters, baby John-John was smearing orange baby food all over his face, and Chad was sitting solemnly, staring at his untouched bowl of spinach, with tears in his eyes.

"You can't get up until you've at least tried it," his father said.

His mother added, "It's really not so bad, kiddo. You should at least taste it."

Chad wasn't sure he could gather up the courage to put a spoonful of the slimy green stuff in his mouth. To him it looked and smelled like something that had come from one of baby John-John's diapers.

"It looks so...*gross*," he said.

"Look, partner," his father said. "You have to eat at least a third of it if you want to get up."

Chad looked up and asked defiantly, "What if I don't?"

His parents looked at one another. "Then you'll sit there until you do."

"What if I'm still sitting here when school starts tomorrow?"

"Then we'll put it in the fridge and you can eat it when you come home," his mother said. "It's not as good cold."

Chad's father made a big show out of eating a spoonful of the green gook. "Look, Chad, it's not bad. Do you think I would eat it if it was gross?"

Chad stared at him. "You eat cow testicles."

His father looked at his mother, who was trying not to laugh.

"Well," his father said, "you're gonna sit there until you eat it, and that's that."

"But," Chad said, "what if I throw it up?"

"Then you'll eat the vomit."

And then they went about their adult conversation.

"I can't believe he's such a monster," Chad's mother said.

Chad looked up, his eyes big. "*Who's* a monster?"

"Your dad's boss, Mr. Greenberg."

Chad wasn't sure he'd heard correctly. "Mr. Greenberg is a monster?"

His father laughed. "Oh, yeah, son. He's a monster all right. He's a real shit head."

"But he's a real-life monster?"

"The worst kind," his mother said, laughing.

"But he looks normal," Chad said, thinking back to all the times he'd seen Mr. Greenberg at his father's softball games. He'd been a terrible pitcher, but he looked like a normal man.

"Most monsters look like normal people," his father said, eating another bite of spinach.

Chad was surprised. *"They do?"*

"Oh, yes," his father said. "They walk amongst us, assholes every one."

Chad looked at his spinach determinedly, dug his spoon in, and scarfed down a full half bowl of the stuff. "Can I get up now?"

His mother and father looked at each other, their mouths hanging open.

Chad went upstairs and telephoned David at once.

"Whatcha doin'?" he asked.

"Watching *Roger Rabbit.*"

"Why?"

"I'm looking at Jessica Rabbit's boobs."

Chad nodded. "They are nice boobs, even if it's just a cartoon."

"What are you doing?" David asked.

"I wanna talk to you about our idea."

"Which idea?"

"The idea of starting our own Monster-Killers Club."

"Okay."

"You still wanna do it?"

"Sure, if we can find some monsters."

Chad beamed. "I know where there's a real-life monster."

"Where?"

"Right here in Maybridge," said Chad.

David was stunned. *"Really?* A real-life monster—*in Maybridge?"*

"Sure."

"Who is it?"

"My Dad's boss, Mr. Greenberg," Chad said. "He's a real-life monster."

"Are you sure?"

"Oh, yeah, my parents told me all about him."

"What does he look like? Is he green? Does he have horns?"

"Nah," said Chad. "He just looks like a normal person."

"Then how do you know he's a monster?"

"Because my Mom and Dad told me. Why would they lie?"

"Hmm. Well, what exactly does he look like?"

"He's kind of fat. And bald. He tries to comb his hair across his bald spot so no one knows he's bald, but you can still tell. My Mom and Dad make fun of him all the time for that."

"They do?"

"Yeah."

"They're not scared of him, him being a monster and all?"

"No, I don't think so. My Dad says he's a shit head."

David laughed at the curse word. "Finally, we have a real-life monster, right here in Maybridge."

"My Mom and Dad say there are others, too."

"Really?"

"Yeah, they say they look just like normal people, too."

"That's not quite as fun, without them having horns and wings and tails and stuff."

"But still."

"Yeah, I guess so," David said. "I wonder if maybe Mr. Dixon, our P.E. teacher, is a monster..."

"Probably not."

"But maybe. So now what?"

"Let's sleep on it," Chad said. "We'll each think about it tonight and then we'll talk about it more tomorrow."

"Sounds good."

The next day in the school lunchroom Chad and David held the first ever official meeting of their incarnation of the Monster-Killers Club. Chad was eating a sack lunch consisting of a pickle loaf sandwich, a baggie full of crunchy Cheetos, a Snickers bar, and a thermos filled with grape juice. David was having the school lunch, which consisted of a barbecue rib patty, a hard roll, questionable mashed potatoes with brown gravy, even more questionable green beans, and a carton of half-frozen chocolate milk.

"Before we get down to business, you wanna trade your barbecue rib patty for my Snickers bar?"

"Is it a regular Snickers bar or the dark chocolate kind?"

"Why?"

"The dark chocolate kind makes me poop."

"Oh," Chad said, examining the candy bar. "Nah, it's the regular kind."

"Okay," David said, handing over the barbecue rib patty on a napkin.

"Now let's talk monsters."

"Okay, shoot."

"We need to exterminate Mr. Greenberg.."

David's eyes lit up. "Yeah, we do."

"How do you wanna do it?"

"What if we take an electrified sword like the one Ben uses and chop off his head? That would be cool."

Chad nodded. "That would be cool, but where are we gonna get an electrified sword?"

"At the pawn shop, maybe?"

"But we don't have any money."

"I got three dollars for watching my little brother while my parents went to the movies."

"I don't think three dollars will buy an electrified sword."

David nodded. "My Daddy has a hunting rifle. Maybe we could just shoot him."

"My Dad says I'm not ever supposed to touch a gun," Chad said earnestly.

"How will he know?"

"I don't know, but I wouldn't feel right about it."

"Okay, hmmm," David said, thinking. "What if we start him on fire?"

"I dunno."

"Why?"

"It seems messy. What if we accidentally spread the fire, or even worse, what if we accidentally start ourselves on fire? How are we gonna explain that?"

"Yeah, but fire is fun."

Chad nodded. "Yeah, fire *is* fun."

"We could drop a safe on him, like in the cartoons."

Chad stared at him. "Did you really just say that?"

David looked at him sheepishly. "Like the cartoons."

"You been watching too much *Roger Rabbit*."

"I guess."

"Wait."

"Okay?"

"What if we kill him just the way Sarah killed the Monster of Palm Springs in issue eight of the comic?" asked Chad.

David thought about it, nodding. "It could work."

"It will work!" Chad said excitedly.

And that was how they determined how they would kill the monster.

It was four-thirty and Tommy Greenberg was just getting off work. He hated working overtime since he was on salary and didn't get paid any extra for it. It had been a long day, and Tommy had gotten his ass chewed out by Mr. Kearns, the regional manager. *Fucking paperwork*. It was *always* paperwork. So, of course, Tommy had had to scream at his employees. Donnie Clemens had caught the brunt of it since he'd been in close proximity after Tommy had gotten off the phone.

Now Tommy was exhausted. It was hard goddamn work screaming at people all day. He knew his stupid employees thought he enjoyed it, but the truth was that he hated it. It just took too much of his energy, leaving him too tired to do anything fun after work.

He was tired now. Probably he would just go home, down a few beers, watch four or five episodes of *Law and Order: SVU*, and jerk off before calling it a night and going to bed. Same old same, every night the same.

Goddamn employees, he thought again, as he opened the door to his Subaru and climbed in. He stuck the key into the ignition and turned it, and both the car and the Dane Cook CD he had in the stereo came blaring to life. "Ever have an itchy ass?" Cook was asking. Tommy laughed at this and stomped on the gas pedal, turned the steering wheel hard, and peeled out of the parking lot.

Chad and David were crouched behind Mr. Greenberg in the backseat of the old Subaru. There was a man on the radio talking about itchy asses, and David, who loved curse words, found himself on the verge of laughter. Chad just stared at him, letting him know that he could easily join this monster in death if he made the wrong move. After all, monster killing was serious business. David got the message loud and clear and forced himself to suppress the laugh.

Mr. Greenberg was driving wildly, and the car was tossing them all around. Chad was right behind him. He started to rise slowly, careful not to be seen by the monster in the front seat. Chad pulled out the screwdriver and raised it slowly. As he did, Mr. Greenberg caught a glimpse of him in the rearview mirror. He turned suddenly, the car swerving sharply as he did, and Mr. Greenberg managed, *"Chad?* Donnie Clemens' boy? What are *you—?"*

Mr. Greenberg swerved hard again, and forced himself to take his eyes off his would-be attacker and turn back to the road. When he did, Chad jammed the screwdriver into the back of Mr. Greenberg's neck, turning it slowly, fighting his way through what felt like hard gristle. Something inside the monster's neck made a grotesque cracking sound.

Mr. Greenberg screamed out, throwing his arms up. *"Arrrrrrgggggghhhhh!"* The now-unattended steering wheel turned sharply to the left and the car jerked. Chad pulled the screwdriver out of the monster's neck and then jammed it hard into the back of his head. Blood shot everywhere. *"Ayyyyeeeeee!"* screamed Mr. Greenberg, his hands clawing at the back of his head. Chad pulled the screwdriver out and jammed it into the monster's head again, just above his neck. The dying monster stomped on the gas pedal and the car was flying now, spinning to the left, and finally coming to an abrupt stop as it struck a tree *hard*. Mr. Greenberg, Chad, and David all shot forward from the impact of the crash. Mr. Greenberg, screwdriver still stuck in the back of his head, lunged violently forward into the steering wheel, and the horn blared for infinity.

Chad and David's heads had struck the back of the seat, splitting open both of their foreheads. Chad looked at David with some confusion, and David started screaming, "I can't see! I'm blind, Chad! I've gone blind!"

"No, no," Chad said calmly. He pulled up David's shirt to wipe away the blood from his face. "You've just got blood in your eyes." Once David could see again, he calmed down a bit.

"Come on," Chad said. "We've got to get out of here."

He opened the door, and the two of them scooted out from the backseat of the wrecked Subaru.

As they walked home, Chad and David each beamed, feeling accomplished as Monster Killers.

"I had fun today," said David, chewing the monster's blood from his fingernails.

"Me too," Chad said.

"We should do this again."

"Oh, yeah, we should *definitely* do this again."

"But before we do," David said, "we should save up our allowances and buy an electrified sword like the one they use on the TV show."

"That would be awesome."

David agreed. "That *would* be awesome."

And the two esteemed Monster Killers walked home in the cold September wind, their faces bloodied, their clothes tattered, and their foreheads split open as trophies of the heroic deed they had committed.

"You know what?" Chad asked.

"What?"

"I'll trade you that comic book for that new *Spider-Man* comic and that *Batman* if you'll throw in your 2008 Topps Derek Jeter All-Star card."

The two of them shook bloody hands. "Deal."

And life was good.

THE SECRET LIFE OF FIRE

Jimmy Reilly was a third-generation FDNY firefighter. He was still a probie when he'd gone to visit his Grandpa Don at St. Pete's nursing home in Flatbush a few years back. That was the day they had the rather strange conversation about fire. It would be their last discussion about anything before Grandpa Don had passed on to the other side, but it would also be one Jimmy would never, ever forget.

His grandfather had served on the FDNY for nearly forty years. The guy was a living legend. Firefighters talked about him with all the reverence a Yankees fan talked about Mickey Mantle, or with which a Christian spoke of Jesus Christ. Grandpa Don had lived a life of hard drinking and excessive risk-taking, and was now a broken-down old codger suffering from dementia. Sometimes he didn't know who or where he was. On this particular day, however, he was as lucid as Jimmy had ever known him to be.

He was sitting in his big Lazy-Boy, leafing through a *TV Guide*, searching for a show that had been canceled for at least a decade, and drinking a can of Ensure from a straw. But this wasn't dementia—it was just Grandpa Don being Grandpa Don.

"I can't find *Murder She Wrote*," he said with no shortage of annoyance.

"They don't make that show no more," Jimmy said.

"I love that Angela Lansbury. She reminds me of your grandma, God rest her soul. Have you seen the tits on Angela Lansbury? Whoa! Reminds me of your grandmother."

The conversation had then (thankfully) turned to firefighting, and despite his now-feeble mind, Grandpa Don had shared tale after tale of his firefighting heroics. Then, interrupting his own story, he said, "I'd like some peach brandy now."

Jimmy said, "I don't think you're supposed to have that."

Before Jimmy could protest any further, Grandpa Don had already pressed the button to call for his nurse. A moment later, an uptight-looking Nurse Ratched-type poked her head into the room. Grandpa Don once again requested peach brandy. The nurse frowned, looking at him like he was an ignorant child. "You know you can't have alcohol in here," she said. She looked at Jimmy. "Your grandfather has been...how shall I say? *Difficult* today."

Jimmy just laughed.

After the nurse left, Grandpa Don said, "Tell you what, Jimmy. You run to the corner store and get me a bottle, I'll tell you the truth about fire."

Jimmy didn't understand. "The truth? About fire?"

"The one thing every old-timer knows, and no one will ever tell you. The secret of the fire."

"What exactly does that mean?"

"Get me a bottle and I'll tell you."

Jimmy figured this was just the ramblings of a half-crazed senior, but nevertheless he went to the corner store and bought his grandfather a bottle. He then returned it to the nursing home, dumped out his grandfather's can of Ensure, and filled it with brandy.

"Thank you, boy," Grandpa Don said, drinking the brandy through an Ensure-crusted straw.

"You said you'd tell me the secret of fire," Jimmy said.

Grandpa Don's eyes had lit up at this. "It's a queer thing, fire. There are things every old fireman knows, but no one dares speak of. That, my boy, is the secret of the fire."

"What kinds of things?"

"Fire is magical," Grandpa Don said. "It can do strange things to a man over time."

"What do you mean?"

"It plays with your mind. Or at least you *think* it's playing with your mind at the time. You work on the job long enough, you start to see things within that fire. Bad things. Unexplainable things. Things you can't explain and probably wouldn't want explained to you if you could."

"I don't understand."

"Stay on this job long enough and you will," Grandpa Don said. "You start seeing the flames dancing to and fro, like creatures swaying to a rhythm only they can hear. You see figures within the fire."

"Figures?" Jimmy asked.

"You're gonna think I'm crazy when I say this, boy, but there are things within the fire that don't always make themselves known. Watch the fire...watch within those flickering flames...and you'll catch glimpses of them."

"Glimpses of what?"

"I don't know exactly," Grandpa Don said. "*Things*. After a while, you'll start to see the fire for what it is—a living, breathing thing. But they hide. The creatures hide within those flames, and it burns the eyes when you stare directly into the fire, searching for them."

Jimmy thought his grandfather had gone back to Cuckoo Town, but humored him just the same.

"You stay on the job long enough, you'll eventually see the creatures for yourself. And that day will change you forever. You'll start to see things differently, and I don't just mean fire. You'll start to comprehend that there are strange and powerful forces in this world that we aren't always aware of. Humans are funny creatures. We think we know everything, but the truth is we only know a little of what exists in this world. There's more out there than just what we can see."

Jimmy asked, "But you've seen the creatures within the fire?"

Grandpa Don grinned a strange little grin, turning to look him in the eyes. "I've seen them with my own eyes, Jimmy, and what a sight it was to behold. They're beautiful, but in the way the sirens who called the sailors onto the rocks were beautiful."

"What do you mean?"

"Fire is dangerous." Grandpa Don laughed. "I know that sounds obvious, but you don't know the half of it, boy. The creature, or creatures, whatever the hell it is, that lurk within those flames, are as dangerous as anything you'll ever encounter in this world or the next. They're the stuff nightmares are made of, and once you've seen their faces, nothing will ever be the same for you."

Jimmy thought about it. "You've seen their *faces*?"

"I saw one. I've seen the whole damned thing, coming towards me out of the belly of the fire. It came to me and tried to pull me into the flames with it. It tried to seduce me into that flickering fire. And you know, for a moment, I almost walked into those flames on my own accord."

Jimmy's eyes grew wide, like he was a small boy listening to a wonderful story. "You did?"

"Almost," Grandpa Don said, holding his hand up to show his thumb and forefinger pulled just a tiny bit apart. "I came this close to walking into that fire and never looking back."

Jimmy didn't know what to say. "Well, I'm glad you didn't."

"So am I. At least I used to be."

"What do you mean?"

"This life here," Grandpa Don said, surveying the room, "isn't much of a life at all. Had I stepped into that fire and danced with that thing, I might've spared myself all this misery. There are days I don't even know what's going on. And their rules here—don't get me started on the rules. I worked my ass of for forty years, I should be able to have a drink or a smoke when I want. But I can't. And that goddamn nurse treats me just like an insolent little brat."

The two of them had talked some more beyond that, covering subjects as diverse as baseball and women, but Jimmy walked away from the conversation thinking only of what his grandfather had told him about the secret of the fire.

Work had kept Jimmy busy, and he didn't get back to see Grandpa Don before his death a month or so later. Grandpa Don's death had been a strange one, and some had speculated that the old man had simply found a unique way to commit suicide.

It was a Tuesday night when Jimmy got the call from his pops, Pat Reilly, also an FDNY legend.

"Jimmy, I got some bad news for ya."

"What's wrong?"

"It's Grandpa Don."

And Jimmy knew. His heart sunk at once, and guilt at not having seen him more frequently began to set in.

"He's dead?" Jimmy asked.

"Yeah."

"Die in his sleep?"

"Not exactly," Pops said.

Jimmy didn't understand. "Well then, how did he die?"

"It's a strange thing."

"What?"

"He died in a fire," Pops said. "Weirdest damn thing. He worked on the job for forty years and then died from a fire inside a nursing home."

Jimmy remembered what his grandfather had told him about fire, but said nothing.

"How did the fire start?" Jimmy asked.

"Well," Pops said, "They think he was smoking a cigar in his room, and you know he wasn't supposed to be smoking, and he accidentally lit himself on fire."

"How is that possible?"

"They think he may have gotten some sort of flammable cleaning solution on his clothing," Pops said. "My guess is it was his goddamn peach brandy... Then, when he dropped that cigar, *whoosh!* The fire started."

Jimmy scratched his head. "Did he die instantaneously?"

"Um," Pops said weakly. "Not exactly. One of the nurses came into the room and said he was standing there, flailing his arms, completely on fire. She said he looked like he was dancing. Hell, even his head and face were on fire, so needless to say, it's gonna be a closed-casket funeral."

A few days later, Jimmy and his his pops had a few drinks at Danny Boy's Tavern after Grandpa Don's funeral. The Reillys drank a lot, and it had been half-joked that their family crest should simply be a bottle of booze. Jimmy and Pops were still dressed in their funeral clothes, sitting on bar stools, each of them downing their poison of choice. For Jimmy it was Jagermeister, and for Pops it was Wild Turkey. They shared a pack of Newports, and they talked fondly about their memories of Grandpa Don.

Finally, once they both were good and sloshed, Jimmy brought up the strange conversation he'd had with Grandpa Don.

"Pops, did Grandpa Don ever say anything strange to you?"

Pops chuckled. "There at the end he said all kinds of crazy shit. One day he told me he was a friggin' space man, so you're gonna have to be more specific, son. What do you mean by strange?"

"He ever say anything weird about fire?"

Pops' smile fell away. "Oh, *that.*"

"You know what I'm talking about?"

"About creatures dancing around in the flames?" Pops asked. "Yeah, he told me about that a couple of times."

"What do you think about it?"

"I think it's crazy-talk," Pops said. "I ain't never seen no man or no creatures or nothing else dancing around in those flames."

"You ever hear anyone else saying something like that?" asked Jimmy.

"Once or twice, from the old-timers. It's just the crazed talk of old men. When I first started on the job, you'd hear whispers around the station from the old guys. Then you'd see it in their eyes, and you'd know what they were thinking as clearly as if they'd said it out loud. But the thing is, it's all bullshit. Sure, the flames flicker and waver and dance, but that's just fire. That's what it does. There's nothing magical living within it. Fire is just fire."

And that was that. The two men, father and son, shared a few more drinks and smokes and nothing else was said about Grandpa Don's story.

It was a Spring afternoon, a tad bit chilly outside, and Jimmy had been on the job for nine years now. His conversation with Grandpa Don was now far behind him in his rearview mirror and Jimmy had long since moved on. He still thought of what his crazy old grandfather had said to him, but he now chalked it up as being nothing more than the loony talk of a man suffering from dementia.

They got the call at just after four. Jimmy was lying on his bunk, reading the latest issue of *Hustler*, when the alarm sounded. He and the rest of the crew hopped to it and boarded their trucks, heading towards an apartment building fire only eight or nine blocks away.

When they got there, Jimmy made his way into the building. The black smoke was billowing out of the place, and it was coming from the second floor. Jimmy and the guys rushed headlong up those stairs towards that fire. They could hear voices screaming up there. Once they reached the top of those stairs, they went their separate ways.

Jimmy knocked on the first apartment door he came to, but no one answered. He then used his ax to chop the door down, and he rushed in through the black smoke. Once he was inside, he could hear screams from the next room, and the crackling sound of fire.

"Don't worry!" he shouted instinctively. "I'm coming in!"

He moved towards the doorway, raised his ax, and chopped through it, finally making it possible to open what was left of the door. The fire was raging hard inside the bedroom, and there was a figure standing just on the other side of the flames, screaming bloody murder. Jimmy could see it was a young black kid, maybe ten years old.

"I'm coming," Jimmy said, looking for a way around the fire.

The flames were on the verge of engulfing the boy, and Jimmy wasn't sure he could reach him without injuring them both. As the flames got closer to the kid, he screamed out ever more loudly.

"I promise," Jimmy said. "I'm coming through to get you."

Jimmy moved towards the fire, now seeing it for what it truly was for the first time. He looked at the boy, and could see the form of a creature—or was it a man?—emerging from the flames now looming over him. The figure's fiery hands reached out for the boy, grabbing him by his bare arms, and the boy cried out in agony.

Jimmy froze for a moment, transfixed by the sight of the fire creature Grandpa Don had detailed. Jimmy moved quickly into the fire, the heat rising up all around him. He quickly approached the young boy, who was now being pulled back slowly into the fire by the flaming figure. The boy was still screaming, trying his hardest to wrestle himself free from the creature's grip, but it was to no avail.

Jimmy reached for the boy. He didn't dare stare directly at the figure, for he now remembered what Grandpa Don had told him about its seductive ways. Jimmy tried to avert his eyes, and he grabbed the boy around his arms. He could feel the grip of the fire creature's hands just above his own, and he pulled the little boy as hard as he could, hoping to save him from being engulfed in flames.

"Jimmy," the fire whispered. "Step into the fire and have a dance."

No, Jimmy thought, tugging at the crying boy with everything he had.

"Come on in, Jimmy. The fire's fine," whispered the flames, sparking and flickering.

And Jimmy managed to pull the young boy free from the creature's grip. He scooped the kid up, turned, and ran through the flames as quickly as he could. He turned back towards the creature for one last glimpse, and he saw it slowly moving back into the flames towards the belly of the fire.

"Jimmy," the fire whispered. "We will meet again."

Jimmy turned and carried the kid down the stairs to safety.

The little boy was in shock and couldn't speak.

"He okay?" Jimmy asked later.

"Damnedest thing," answered Captain Collins. "The kid had burn marks on his arms. Thing is, they looked like hand prints."

"That's strange," Jimmy said.

But Jimmy now knew the truth about life and fire. He knew there was more to this world than what could be seen with the naked eye, and he knew if one looked closely enough he or she might see something unexpected within the darkness of the shadows or the bright light of the fire.

He also knew one day he would meet up again with the figures in the flames, formidable adversaries to be sure. He'd won today, but he'd been lucky. He vowed that next time he would be ready for the creatures, whatever the hell they were.

CAPTAIN MARVELOUS SAVES THE WORLD

Alex always knew one day he'd be a superhero. He hadn't been born with any super-powers to speak of, but he'd been fascinated with superheroes since he'd read his first issue of Batman at age six. After college, he briefly considered relocating to Los Angeles to become one of the professional superheroes who hang out and take pictures with fans in front of Grauman's Chinese Theatre. But then he had thought the better of it. Why settle for being a glorified panhandler when you could be a real superhero? He'd then looked around at his hometown Chicago and realized there was enough criminal activity here to keep a superhero in business for a good long time.

That was when he developed his superhero alter-ego Captain Marvelous. He had initially planned to use the iconic red, white, and blue colors that Captain America wore, but wound up settling for something a tad bit different. Each night when he stalked crime in the streets of Chi Town, Alex donned silky black tights, a red and black Dracula cape, and a red Lucha Libre mask he'd purchased for five bucks at a flea market downtown. He would study himself proudly in his bedroom mirror each night, dressed as Captain Marvelous, surrounded by the posters, photographs, and toys of famous Marvel and DC superheroes who inspired him.

Nobody in high school would have imagined that Alex would become anything spectacular. If they had taken a vote, he might have been selected Most Likely to Work As a Janitor. Sure, he worked as a short order cook in a diner downtown, but at night he was a superhero.

He was Captain Marvelous, crime-fighter.

Other classmates from school had gone on to bigger and better things. Timmy Voss had become a real-estate magnate worth a billion dollars. John

Chase had gone on to write a dozen or so bestselling crime thrillers that had been adapted into major motion pictures. And Tony Scoggins, an old high school chum of Alex's, had gone on to win an Emmy for a short-lived cop show no one remembered anymore. Those were all respectable endeavors to be sure, but Alex felt he had outdone them by becoming a professional superhero. Of course no one could know his true identity, so he hung out with no one and spoke only to his parents. Maybe no one knew Alex was Captain Marvelous, but he knew it, and that was enough to make him proud.

After all, what was a nobler endeavor than being a superhero? Superheroes were America. Maybe they didn't really exist—at least not prior to Alex establishing Captain Marvelous—but Alex believed they were as American as apple pie and afternoon ball games at Wrigley. Alex was just carrying on the proud tradition set forth in the yellowed pages of comics like The Spectacular Spider-Man, The Amazing X-Men, and The Fantastic Four. Alex liked to dream of a Captain Marvelous comic. Maybe someday, if he did his job well enough, such a thing would exist.

But for now Alex couldn't concern himself with such trivialities. Now he had to focus on the task at hand, and that was being a superhero and fighting crime wherever it lurked within those deep and dark shadows of the city. For where there was crime, there would be one man there to stop it—Captain Marvelous.

Alex was standing in front of the mirror again, admiring his Captain Marvelous garb and thinking grandiose thoughts about his life as a crime-fighter. He pulled on his Bears coat over his suit and took off the Lucha Libre mask. This way he could leave his house without being noticed. He then climbed into his old Cavalier and made his way into the city.

Watch out crime, Captain Marvelous was on the prowl.

He pulled up just off Rush Street, and sat in his car watching the hookers make their way up and down the street for several minutes. He looked around, but saw no pimp. He then turned on a side street with more hookers on it, and he saw a black man wearing a gaudy purple fedora, Elvis sunglasses, a big white coat made from some type of animal's fur, and several gold rope necklaces. The man was standing in the center of the block, holding court, surrounded by three or four hookers (two of which looked like trannys).

Alex pulled off into the next alley down from where the pimp was. He left the keys dangling in the ignition—he wouldn't be gone long—and started back down the poorly-lit street towards the pimp. Neither the pimp nor the hookers milling around seemed to pay him much mind, despite his wearing a mask. But then, when Alex was less than ten feet from the pimp, one of the hookers noticed him.

"What the hell, man?" "she" said in a thick Latino accent.

The other hookers started to mumble amongst themselves.

The pimp just smiled, "Who you supposed to be?"

Alex grinned. "Are you a pimp?"

Now it was the pimp's turn to grin. "Well, I ain't running a lemonade stand."

"That's what I thought."

Alex stepped towards the pimp forcefully, and the girls instinctively backed away. Alex's hand was on the handle of his Captain Marvelous machete now. He slid it out of its scabbard and swung it at the pimp hard, cutting off at least most of his left arm. It was difficult to determine the full extent of the damage because of the pimp's oversized white fur coat, which was quickly turning red now. The pimp was just standing there screaming, staring down at his severed arm. Alex pulled back the machete again, and brought it swooping in towards the pimp. The blade slid smoothly into the side of the pimp's neck, but got stuck midway through at the Adam's apple. The pimp just stood there, convulsing, the blade sticking out of his throat. Alex pulled the machete out of the pimp's neck, and the pimp's body fell to the pavement with a loud thud. Alex looked at the hookers, now fleeing down the street in the opposite direction, and turned back towards his vehicle. He made his way quickly down the street towards the alley, made the turn, and saw the Cavalier there. He climbed inside, pulled the door shut, and got the hell out of there.

Later that night, Alex was staring at himself in the mirror in his Captain Marvelous suit. The TV was playing in the background, but Alex paid it no mind. A news reporter was breaking in with an emerging story that the serial killer known as the Night Slayer had struck again that night, apparently chopping someone up with some sort of sword or machete. But Alex was oblivious to this. He was too busy admiring himself in the mirror and dreaming of his superhero exploits from earlier in the night.

"This now brings the Night Slayer's death toll up to nine," the reporter was saying.

Alex took off his Lucha Libre mask and stared into the mirror, feeling pride in himself and his work as a crime-fighter. He wished he could tell his parents about his alter-ego and all the nine criminals he had stopped, as he badly wanted to share his pride with someone else. Seeing them look upon him with admiration of their own would be a plus.

This was the downside of being a superhero—not being able to tell anyone. Here Alex was, doing God's work if ever anyone had done so, and no one would ever know a thing about it. He had to worry about keeping himself and his family safe. If the criminals knew who he was, they'd come after him at his home. He'd seen it in the comics. They'd come after his Mom and Dad and hold them hostage or maybe even kill them. And Alex couldn't have that. He couldn't put innocent lives in jeopardy. This was just the way it was. This was the life of a superhero.

Alex waited a few nights before going back out into the streets. He never went out on consecutive nights. He liked to keep the criminals on their toes, so they'd never know when to expect him. Besides, it was too risky to go out and catch bad guys every single night of the week.

So here he was again, rolling through the nighttime streets of Chicago in his little teal 1993 Cavalier in search of crime. Finally he spotted an obvious drug transaction going down in the old Cabrini-Green area. He pulled the Cavalier up to the curb across the street and waited for the buyer to leave. The street was dark. The man purchasing the drugs was a black guy, and the drug dealer was some little white hipster-looking douche bag. Once the buyer moved on, Alex climbed out of the car and took off his Bears coat, revealing his Captain Marvelous suit. He then pulled on his mask and approached the drug dealer.

"Can I help you with something?" the drug dealer asked. "You don't look like you're from around here."

"Yeah," said Alex. "I need to score some meth."

The drug dealer chuckled. "What do I look like, a friggin' pharmacy?"

"I got money."

The drug dealer looked down the street. "All right, let's see the cash."

Alex came up with the machete and sliced it across the man's abdomen, his entrails starting to fall out. The man cried out in pain and looked down at his stomach, trying to hold his innards in.

"Crime doesn't pay," Alex said.

The drug dealer looked up at him. "Who the fuck are you?"

"I'm Captain Marvelous."

And Alex brought the machete swooping in towards the man's temple, burying the blade in his skull. The machete made a sickening chunk! noise as it struck. The drug dealer's eyes rolled up into his stupid hipster head, and he fell to the pavement with a thud.

Alex looked down at his work proudly.

Captain Marvelous had done it again.

Captain Marvelous ten, bad guys zero.

He looked both ways, saw no one in either direction, and made his way quickly back to the car. He climbed in, pulled off the mask, and started the ignition. He drove away into the night, once again feeling accomplished.

The television was playing behind him once again as Alex admired himself in his mirror, but there was no update on the Night Slayer's latest victim. The television wouldn't report that little factoid until Alex was in the restroom, out of earshot. The report wouldn't end until after Alex was finished, saving him from hearing the story.

Alex waited almost a week before going out to battle the city's criminals once again. When he did, he could find no crime and had to give up for the night. He then waited two more nights before going out and scouring the streets again. This time he saw a young Puerto Rican man in a camouflaged Army jacket fleeing from a liquor store robbery with a pistol in his hand. Hearing police sirens in the far-off distance, Alex slowly tracked the robber, his headlights off.

The robber made a big, rounding turn around the next corner. Alex stomped on the gas. He'd be damned if he was gonna let this criminal get away from the justice he so rightfully deserved. When Alex came screeching around the corner in the Cavalier, the running robber turned back and fired a shot at him, cracking the windshield. Alex sped up, got right up on him, and jumped the curb, forcing the robber back out into the street. The robber stumbled over the curb and fell. Alex hit him hard with the car. Then he backed up, making sure the guy was pinned under his tires.

Alex came up out of the car.

"You made a big mistake," said Alex.

The man looked at him through bloodied eyes, squirming in pain. "Who are you?"

"I'm the judge and the jury," Alex said. "I'm Captain Marvelous."

Alex moved in and pulled out the machete, bringing it up over his head. He brought the thing slicing straight down into the top of the robber's head, and blood sprayed everywhere. The blade stuck in the man's head, just above his eyebrows. Alex pulled the machete free, and chopped the man's neck against the asphalt. The head almost came completely off, just a flap of skin and a couple of tendons holding it there, dangling off to one side.

Hearing the sirens growing nearer and nearer, Alex reached down and scooped up the sack of money the robber had dropped into the street.

"To the victor go the spoils," he said. He then climbed into the car and drove away. Alex smiled at himself in the rearview mirror.

Yes, life was good.

Alex was a superhero, out here in the streets doing God's work.

Late that night, Alex sat on the corner of his bed, watching television and eating a big bowl of garlic popcorn with hot sauce. A news story interrupted the episode of Leave It to Beaver he was watching. The reporter informed viewers that the Night Slayer had struck again, dismembering his eleventh victim after running over him with a car.

Alex nodded, a wide grin on his face.

A serial killer, he thought. The fucking Night Slayer.

Yes, Captain Marvelous had finally found a suitable arch-enemy in Chi-Town.

Alex looked into the mirror again, still wearing the Captain Marvelous suit sans the mask. He smiled at himself, promising that one day he would catch this so-called Night Slayer and give him exactly what he deserved.

CUT AND RUN

The waves on the lake were growing choppier and choppier, but Sam didn't much notice. He'd been drinking beer since nine in the morning, and now, eleven hours later, he was feeling no pain. Here was out on his big twenty-foot Cobalt ski boat, alone, and still having the time of his life.

He didn't do much skiing these days—not since Lisa had left him for his best friend, Jerry. He really had no other friends to speak of, and with Lisa and Jerry both gone, there was no one left for him to ski behind. So instead Sam just sat out in the summer sun, drinking beer and listening to music all day. Sometimes he would jump into the water to go for a cool swim or to take a leak.

He was sitting in this little cove with his anchor dropped, listening to oldies radio, and downing beer after beer. He liked to read on the boat. Right now he was in the middle of Bukowski's *Ham on Rye*, but had been forced to give the book a break once he'd become too inebriated to comprehend it.

It was just after eight when it started to rain. It came down somewhat softly at first, but Sam sensed it would escalate quickly. He was still a good half hour away from the marina where he kept his boat, so he would have to really book to get out of the storm. He pulled up the weighted anchor and sat it aside.

It was starting to get dark, mostly because of the rain. The waves were growing choppier by the minute. Sam had always prided himself on being a good driver, so he maneuvered his way out of the empty cove, going top speed. Paul Revere and his Raiders were on the radio singing "Cherokee Nation," just above the din of the boat's whirring motor. Sam was still drinking beer, downing a third of the can per swig, and tapping his fingers on the steering wheel as he headed back to the marina.

He now had the boat wide-open out in the middle of the lake. The rain was picking up, and the tiny droplets were now zipping in at him like tiny pellets, stinging when they hit. He still had his sunglasses on, which at least protected his eyes, but the wind tore off his baseball cap, leaving it somewhere in his wake.

CCR was now on the radio, singing "Fortunate Son." Sam reached down for the volume knob, turning it up a bit more, even though the cheap speakers were buzzing, already on the verge of blowing out.

Fuck it, Sam thought. After all, he loved Creedence Clearwater Revival, and they were his goddamn speakers to blow if he felt so inclined.

He sang along with old John Fogarty, sounding drunk and loud as he did, and the boat continued to pierce the high waves at an ungodly speed, skimming along like a powerful pebble.

Sam found himself craving another BBQ beef sandwich, despite everything going on around him. The rain was steadily pouring into the boat at an incline, the Cobalt was zipping along, and the radio was blaring to the point of distortion. Sam reached down for the cooler sitting in the center of the boat. It was turned away from him, so it took a moment of fumbling to get the damned thing open and retrieve his sandwich.

Sam looked up and in the briefest flash saw something in the water just ahead of the boat.

It was a person, floating there.

A young woman.

Sam had just barely registered her horrified expression when the ski boat crushed its way over it. Within a second, there came the chomping sound of the propeller tearing through flesh and blood.

And like that, it was over.

Sam looked down at the wrapped-up sandwich, and then back out at the lake, trying to comprehend this terrible thing he'd done.

Sam slowed down the boat, horrified. He swung the thing back around to locate her, knowing full well no one could have survived that. Between the darkness and the rain, he could see nothing.

Shit, he thought. *I gotta call Lake Patrol. I gotta tell someone.*

And then Sam looked down at all the empty beer cans rolling around on the floor, and knew at once he couldn't do that. If they gave him the breathalyzer, he'd be fucked and good, storm or no storm.

The best thing he could do now was to put as much distance between that mangled corpse and himself as possible. No one would find the body for another day with the storm being what it was, and by then the fish would have eaten away at it significantly enough that there should no longer be any clues to be found. And who knew, maybe it would sink...

Why the fuck was there a person way out here alone anyway?

Sam felt his stomach rolling over, warm vomit rising in his throat. He couldn't stop himself. He leaned over and heaved BBQ beef and stale beer all over himself and the inside of the boat.

He turned the boat back around towards the marina, and gunned the thing.

When Sam had the boat tied back inside its slip at the marina, he looked around both ways to make sure no one was around. The marina was empty, and the lights were dim. He filled the cooler with the empty beer cans, so he could remove them without being seen. He then went about cleaning the vomit from the driver's seat and dashboard. Once he was finished, he leaned over the front of the boat, looking down at its hull, to see if the accident had left any tell-tale signs there. It had not. He then walked back and inspected the motor and prop, making sure there was no blood or loose chunks of hair or brain matter there.

Feeling satisfied that no one would ever know what he'd done, Sam carried the cooler out to the parking lot and sat it in the back of his pickup truck. He wasn't happy with himself, but he thought he just might get away with it.

The first night was the worst. He had nightmare upon nightmare about the incident in which he could see glimpses of her face, and woke up several times in the night, soaked in a cold sweat. He would get up and stare at himself long and hard in the mirror, contemplating what he'd done. Again he considered turning himself in to the authorities, but he knew he would never make it in prison. He had seen *Oz*, and he knew what kinds of things happened to soft, middle-aged white men behind those bars.

The second night was a little easier.

The third night even more so.

And so on.

Sam never saw any reports on the news about the dead girl, and no one ever came to ask him about any of it.

And eventually, life went on as normal and Sam rarely ever gave the incident a second thought.

It was a year to the day of the accident. Sam didn't think directly about it, but he was aware of what the day was because it also marked one year of sobriety. He'd had a long day, and thought he'd relax for a bit before heading to bed.

He ran a hot bath, filling the water with bubble bath oil. He knew it wasn't very manly for a forty-five-year-old man to sit in a bubble bath, but he didn't care. He had loved bubble baths since he was a kid, and they always seemed to make him feel at his most relaxed.

Once the water and the bubbles were about two-thirds of the way to the top, Sam climbed into the big tub, thinking it was one of the best investments he'd ever made. He allowed himself to slide down a bit, lying back against the tub, with his legs splayed apart and his feet propped up out of the water on the outer edges of the tub. The bubbles were growing higher and higher, and the water temperature was perfect.

Sam reached down for his one-year-sobriety-celebratory-beer and took a swig. He sat the can down on the edge of the tub, reached over, and picked up his book from the floor, cracking it open. He was attempting to read *Infinite Jest* for the third time. He was only a third of the way through it, and was already struggling.

As he read, he felt something brush against the inside of his thigh. He lowered the book and looked down, seeing something black slowly rising from the bubbles between his legs.

It looked like...*hair!*

Sam was stupefied by what he was seeing, and found himself unable to avert his eyes. There was nowhere for him to go had the thought occurred to him, but at the moment it had not and all of his muscles were locked up in fear anyway.

He watched in terror as a woman's misshapen head with long, stringy black hair, rose slowly up from his bubble bath. As the bubbles fell, he could see her skin was wrinkled, half-eaten, and falling away. Her flesh was an inhumanly bluish-green color. More bubbles fell away and Sam could see a huge, gaping hole in the side of her head, bits of brain dangling out, soapy bubbles resting on them.

Now the distinct smell of fish intertwined with the lilac aroma of his bubble bath.

The dead girl continued to rise out of the water, and now her entire face was visible except for what was hidden by foamy white bubbles. She only had one eye, which was now rotten and translucent. The other had been chewed out of its socket.

Once she rose up past her neck, which was also badly torn apart, Sam could see she was wearing a life jacket.

And it struck him that this was *her.*

But it can't be.

But it was.

He felt his bladder let go, but could do nothing other than acknowledge the fact.

Sam looked to his right and now saw that there were literally a half dozen of the rotten, blue-green corpses just standing there in the doorway, watching through dark, empty eye sockets. One of them reached out and knocked over the scented candle sitting on the sink, and flames rose from the floor at once.

He looked back at the dead girl in the bath tub.

She was now raised out of the water to her waist. She plunged her fist into Sam's mouth, some of her skin scraping off against his teeth, the sickening flavor of her rotten flesh making him feel as though he might vomit. She wrapped her dead, bloated fingers around his tongue, and started pulling it out of his mouth slowly. Sam could feel it ripping, but found he could do nothing to stop it. He reached for her arm in terror, but she was too strong for him.

The dead girl pulled her fist back out of Sam's mouth and held the bloody, severed tongue up to her one remaining eye, examining it. She flicked it aside, and it dropped into the soft white bubbles.

She raised her hand back behind her head and brought her fist swooping in, ramming it through Sam's chest. He could feel her cold hand wrapped around his still-beating heart, and she yanked the organ out, blood spraying all over her face. She held it up in front of Sam's eyes, and for the briefest of seconds he got to see his own heart before he died.

THE RIPPER RETURNS

Mika loved flea markets, so when she had a chance to visit Bernie's Bazaar in Hanover, she couldn't pass on the opportunity. A pack rat by nature, Mika loved to buy things she didn't need as long as she was getting them at a discount. Past purchases included countless paperback books that would never get read, a framed poster of the movie *White Zombie*, which sat in her closet, gathering dust, and a miniature Coke machine that didn't work which now sat in the garage in a pile of junk.

Mika was in town for her mother's stupid doctor's appointment, and she had only two goals while she was in Hanover: to shop at the flea market and eat lunch somewhere interesting. Once the doctor's appointment was concluded, Mika dragged her mother to a little greasy-spoon called Crazy Taco. Then, after the meal, they went shopping at Bernie's Bazaar.

"I don't know why you like these places so much," her mother said. "It's just a glorified garage sale."

Mika rolled her eyes, already tired of her mother. "It's like a hundred different garage sales under one roof. How can you beat that?"

Her mother just said, "Hrumph," examining an empty Elvis Presley whiskey decanter. "Can you believe they want twenty bucks for this piece of crap?"

Mika ignored her mother's bitching.

She then came across a booth filled with old paperbacks. Bingo! This would be the bulk of her day's haul. She perused the books for a while, finally walking away with a small stack of them. Three of them were tattered Stephen King books, one was a copy of Whitley Streiber's *Communion*, and the other was a book on Jack the Ripper, which was in fairly nice condition for the dollar it brought.

Mika then looked through some old comic books. She found a few reprints of *Tales from the Crypt* and *Vault of Horror,* but couldn't bring herself to part with ten bucks per copy. There were also some Archie and Jughead comics which caught her eye, for reasons unbeknownst to her. They were pricey too, so Mika moved on to the next booth.

She then looked through several stacks of old records. A bit of an eccentric, Mika loved vinyl. She wound up picking out a couple of George Carlin comedy albums which were selling for two bucks apiece.

Mika's final purchase came from a booth selling old board games. There she found an old Ouija board, still in great condition, for ten bucks. She had never actually seen a Ouija board up close and in person, and she knew at once this was a unique item she could not pass up.

"Why in god's name are you buying that awful thing?" her mother asked.

"What's the matter with it?"

Her mother said, "Messing with those things is a sin against god. They open a person up to all kinds of evil."

Mika really wished her mother wasn't here with her. "Tell you what: I'll keep it around so I can talk to you after your dead."

"With you around," her mother said, "that might not be too far off."

Mika just ignored her mother and went about her business, looking at some old stamps and coins, a few Twinkies box cut-out baseball cards, and some cheap topaz jewelry she wouldn't be caught dead in. She sneered at a booth of gaudy, homemade grandma sweaters with snowmen sewn on them. Finally, after having spent just under two hours in the place, Mika was ready to check out.

"About time," her mother said. "I could have been home watching *Jeopardy* by now."

Again with the complaining.

"Cool your jets, woman," said Mika. "*Jeopardy* isn't going anywhere. Besides, look at this haul I got."

"Goodie," she said. "More junk to go along with your collection."

Mika took the items to the cash register and sat them on the glass counter. Bernie rang up each item. Bernie tried to overcharge Mika by a dollar, but she quickly caught the mistake. The correct total was just under twenty bucks.

"Not bad," Mika said, proud of her purchases. She paid the man with a twenty, took her change, and the two women left the flea market.

"You're gonna be one of those hoarders, like on TV, one of these days," her mother said. "I can just feel it."

Would you just shut the fuck up? Mika thought.

They both climbed into her little green Volkswagon bug and sped away, homeward bound.

On the forty-five minute ride home, Mika's mother persistently pushed the issue of her dating life, or lack thereof.

"You're a pretty girl," her mother said. "You should have a boyfriend."

"I don't want a boyfriend. Not right now."

"Why?"

Because I'm a lesbian, is what she wanted to say.

But she didn't.

Instead she said, "I don't have time for that right now."

"I know you're still young," her mother said, "but you'll be thirty before you know it. You have no idea how difficult it is for a woman older than thirty to find a man. Look at your father. All older men want is young little perky things like that whore Trisha. I'm telling you, you have a better chance of curing cancer than you do landing a good man after the age of thirty."

"You've told me all this before. Several times, in fact."

"I know," her mother said, "but I'm not sure it's sinking in."

Mika had heard all this bullshit before, and was quite tired of it.

"Next you're gonna say you have life experiences and I should listen to you."

"Well, I *do* have life experiences," her mother said, "and you *should* listen to me. Both those things are true."

Mika picked up her iPod and asked, "What do you wanna listen to?"

"I don't know. You don't have any of the old stuff." Her mother thought for a moment and then asked, "Do you have any Elvis?"

"I've got Elvis Costello."

"*Elvis Costello?* I don't even know who that is."

"You wouldn't."

Mika selected a loud death metal song, just to irk her mother.

The song came blaring on.

"What the hell is this?" her mother asked. "This...this isn't even music."

Mika just smiled, satisfied by her mother's displeasure.

That night Mika cooked herself some spaghetti and sat on the couch, watching *American Psycho* for the umpteenth time. When it was over, she found that she wasn't quite tired enough to go to bed yet. She looked over and noticed the bag of books she had purchased at Bernie's Bazaar sitting there beside the couch. She reached down and picked up the bag, going through it. She had read the three Stephen King books before, so she was already familiar with them. She sat them aside. She then came to the Jack the Ripper book. It was titled *The Diary of Jack the Ripper: The Chilling Confessions of James Maybrick*. She'd never heard of James Maybrick before, so she opened the book and looked through it.

She was hooked at once. The book—an alleged diary—had supposedly been penned by this guy Maybrick, and he alleged in sort of a vague, roundabout way that he had been the famed 1880s English serial killer Jack the Ripper. Of course the authenticity of the book was suspect, but Mika was fascinated by the picture it painted. Her reading was soon interrupted when her cat, Mr. Bond, jumped on her lap. She sat the book down and started petting the purring feline, soon forgetting about the book altogether.

But later that night, as she lay in bed in the darkness of her room, she remembered it. She wondered if its story was true. And if it was true, then how come she'd never heard of this Maybrick guy before?

Her thoughts then moved on to other things, like her ex-girlfriend Holly and the residual pain she still felt from her acts of betrayal. She lay there for hours, unable to sleep, her mind turning, going from subject to subject, and ultimately landing once again on Jack the Ripper. She considered the Maybrick claim for some time. And then she had another thought; she remembered the Ouija board lying on the table downstairs, and thought it might be fun to try and contact James Maybrick through a seance. Sure, she knew Ouija boards didn't work, knew seances were bullshit, but what could it hurt? No one would have to know. Besides, it was two in the morning and she was wide-awake and bored.

Mika got up and went downstairs to retrieve the board. She brought it back upstairs and sat it on her bed. She sat facing the thing, sitting Indian-style. She took the planchette out of its box, and sat it on the board. She then put her hands on the planchette and moved it around the board, across the numbers, and then across the alphabet.

She didn't know where to start.

"Hello?" she said.

The sound of her own voice startled her.

She continued to move the piece around the board.

"Is anyone out there?"

She kept moving the planchette, but felt no pull.

"Hello?"

This time the piece pulled within her hands, dragging itself to the word HELLO. She felt a chill run down her spine. She was more than a little freaked out. But then she started second-guessing the thing, wondering if she had subconsciously moved the piece herself. Yes, of course. That was it. That had to be what happened.

And she spoke again. "Is someone there?"

The planchette once again moved within her hands, swirling around the board, finally landing on the word YES.

"Who are you?" she asked.

The planchette stirred once again, this time dragging itself to the letter "D." It did not move any further.

"D?" she asked. "Is that your name?"

The piece moved within her hands, sliding itself back to the word YES.

"Can you help me find someone?" she asked.

The piece moved around the board again, finally coming to rest back on the word YES.

Mika was still stunned by the movement of the Ouija piece, but now seriously believed it was being moved by her own subconscious. After all, what other explanation could there possibly be? Ouija boards were mass-produced pieces of shit, nothing more than a simple board game. There was no way they worked. Second, Mika didn't believe in goblins, ghosts, and ghoulies. She thought the concept was cool, sure, but she found the existence of such things to be highly unlikely. She considered herself an agnostic, but found the idea of god to be much more believable than the idea of ghosts who just sat out there waiting to be contacted through board games.

Still, the planchette was moving.

At least she thought it was moving.

Maybe she was just nuts.

Yes, that's it, she thought. *I'm certifiable.*

"James Maybrick," she said.

The planchette did not move.

"That's who I'm looking for—James Maybrick."

The Ouija piece started moving within her fingers again, swirling slowly around the board. Finally, after a minute or so, it rested on YES.

"Yes?" Mika asked. "You can help me find James Maybrick?"

And the planchette was on the move again, faster this time, going to the letter "H." It then went to the letter "E." From there it continued to the letter "R." And then it moved to the letter "E," stopping there.

"Here?" asked Mika. "James Maybrick is here?"

The planchette shook a little in her hands, and then slid to YES.

Mika couldn't believe she was doing this. It just seemed so...silly. But nevertheless she pressed on.

"Hello, Mr. Maybrick."

The planchette now slid to the word HELLO.

"I have a question for you."

The planchette did not move.

"Are you Jack the Ripper?"

There was a long enough pause that Mika thought there would be no response, and then, suddenly, she felt the planchette pulling itself towards the word NO.

"You aren't Jack the Ripper?"

The planchette sat still over the word NO.

Even though Mika knew the planchette wasn't really moving, that there was no real James Maybrick spirit here, she still felt somewhat disappointed by the answer she'd received.

"How are you?" she asked, not knowing what else to say.

The planchette sat still for a moment before moving to spell out the word DEAD.

Mika smiled. What else was he gonna say? "How are you?" The guy was dead. That's how he was. What a stupid question.

She was now tired of this game, tired of her subconscious maneuvering the planchette around the board, so she said simply, "Goodbye." The piece moved under her fingertips again, moving to the word GOODBYE.

And that was it.

Mika put the board and planchette back inside their box and put the lid on over them. That had been fun, had killed some time, and now she was ready for bed once again. She turned off the light and lay down on her bed, quickly slipping into a deep sleep. And when she slept, she dreamed she was Jack the Ripper.

The next morning when Mika woke up, she had no memory of her dreams. But she knew there was something different. She couldn't quite put her finger on what it was, but she felt out of sorts. Something was amiss.

Nevertheless, the day would be a normal one, every bit as mundane as those which had preceded it. She went to work at the library, working her shift from nine to five. She noticed nothing out of the ordinary there, but did have a terrible headache pulsing within her temples all day. It wasn't like her to have headaches, and no amount of Ibuprofen seemed to calm it. This one was a doozy.

It was just after seven and she was watching a documentary about the *New York Times* crosswords puzzle when her phone rang. She looked, and saw it was her ex-girlfriend Holly. She knew the phone call would probably be something bad, but she still felt herself growing dangerously optimistic that Holly had seen the error of her ways and was coming back.

"Hello?" she answered.

"Hi, Mika," said Holly. "We need to talk."

Mika missed Holly, but found that she had also grown to loathe her.

"About what?" asked Mika.

"The cat."

Mika looked down at Mr. Bond. "What about him?"

"I want him to come live with me and Karen."

"What?"

"I paid for the little fucker."

"Yeah," Mika said, "but he was a gift. You bought him for me for my birthday."

"But we're not together anymore."

"So you just want to take your gift back?"

"Yeah."

"That makes you an...Indian giver." Mika knew that sounded stupid, but it had just come out.

"So what?"

"But you haven't even come by to see Mr. Bond in months," Mika said. "He's a living, breathing animal. He's not just some inanimate thing you take back whenever you feel like it."

The conversation went on like this for some time, with Holly not listening to reason. In the end, Holly was more determined than ever to take Mr. Bond back, and Mika ended the call in tears.

Then she heard the voice, somewhere deep down inside her head.

You know what you need? the voice asked.

Mika did not answer. After all, this was just some disconnected voice inside her brain.

I know what will make you feel better, the voice said. And Mika knew—it was the voice of James Maybrick, somewhere deep down inside her. Had he possessed her through the Ouija board? Was such a thing possible? She now knew it must be. She could feel him there, sharing the same space within her. She could almost smell his warm, heavy breath on her own. He was a part of her now, the two of them somehow intertwined, sharing the same body.

I know what you need.

The two of them were so interconnected that Mika knew the words before Maybrick could even say them.

I know what you need.

Mika felt her body moving, felt herself going to the kitchen. She was now powerless to stop herself. She saw her hand moving in front of her, reaching for a steak knife. She knew where this was all going, but could do nothing to stop it.

She couldn't even scream out within herself.

Now there was only Maybrick's voice.

She could feel the weight of the knife in her hand, but it felt foreign, as if it was someone else's hand. And in a way it was. Her body was his now to do with as he wished. She could not stop him. Mika was a slave to Maybrick.

Everything will be better soon, he told her.

Mika did as Maybrick willed her to do, and sidled the VW bug up alongside the curb about ten feet from where the hooker was standing. Before Mika even knew what was happening, she felt her body moving, climbing out of the car, her hand wrapped tightly around the handle of the knife in her pocket.

"What you want, sweetie?" asked the hooker. Although the prostitute was probably only thirty or so, she looked much older. She had the look of someone who had once been attractive in a leathery, truck stop sort of way.

"You like girls, huh?" the hooker asked, smiling.

Mika moved in towards her.

"How much?" Mika asked.

The hooker said, "For a nice girl like you—"

Her words were cut short when the blade of the knife penetrated her lower abdomen just above her cunt. The woman made a screeching sound, tried to reach for the knife, but Mika moved quickly, yanking the knife upward, disemboweling her.

Maybrick moved Mika's hand down to the dying hooker's neck, pulling the blade across it, creating a long, smiling gash. Mika could feel the warm blood on her hands, and found herself enjoying it. Maybrick was inside her, corrupting her, recreating her in his own image.

Mika felt her body straighten, and she stared down at the dead prostitute, a pool of blood reaching out further and further from the body.

And Mika felt the smile creeping across her lips, and she wondered if it was hers or Maybrick's.

I gave you what you needed, Maybrick said.

Fully under his control, Mika returned to the car and climbed in. She dropped the thing into drive and sped away.

When Mika got home, she found Holly waiting for her on her porch. Still under Maybrick's control, Mika walked up onto the porch, dried blood on her hands and in her hair.

"I've been waiting for an hour," said Holly.

Mika wanted to tell her to fuck off. She wanted to say that she had a life, too, and had more important things to do than sit at home and wait for the twat to come by whenever she felt like it. She wanted to tell her that Mr. Bond would never go to live with her and her stupid girlfriend.

But she said none of this, as Maybrick wouldn't allow it.

Instead, she approached Holly, getting right up in her face.

Holly's expression changed. "Is that blood on your cheek?"

Mika felt her hand jutting out before her, the blade sinking itself into the stomach of her ex-lover. Holly made a loud gasping sound, and then started to vomit a little. Maybrick yanked Mika's hand upward, disemboweling Holly with a single rip.

And as Mika cut up her dying ex-girlfriend, she felt herself slipping back into that old familiar feeling. It was then she remembered that Jack the

Ripper had only killed prostitutes. And she knew James Maybrick was just a lie she told herself so she wouldn't have to face her own demons.

Mika slashed Holly's throat, and blood seeped out everywhere.

Mika grinned, wiping her face with a bloody hand.

If Maybrick was a fiction, she vowed to go on feeding herself this lie. She'd already buried memories of the past, so forgetting this should be no problem. Maybrick would be alive and well inside her. She would forever be a slave to him, her actions not her own.

After all, he knew what she needed.

ABOUT THE AUTHOR

Andy Rausch is a freelance journalist, celebrity interviewer, and film critic. He is the author or co-author of nearly twenty books on the subject of popular culture. These include *Making Movies with Orson Welles*, *The Films of Martin Scorsese and Robert De Niro*, and *The Wit and Wisdom of Stephen King*. He is also the author of the novels *Elvis Presley, CIA Assassin, Mad World* and *Bloodletting*. He has also worked as an actor, film producer, composer, casting director, and as the screenwriter of the cult film *Dahmer vs. Gacy*. He is a regular contributor to *Screem* magazine, and his work has appeared in such publications and online journals as *Film Threat*, *Shock Cinema*, and *Bright Lights Film Journal*. He resides in Parsons, Kansas.

MAD WORLD BY ANDY RAUSCH

"*Mad World* is dark, twisted, no-holds-barred fun."
—Jason Starr, author of *Bust*, *Slide*, and *The Max*

EVERYONE'S PLAYING AN ANGLE IN THE CITY OF ANGELS

Mad World tells the stories of a black hitman who doubles as a university professor, a Catholic priest who longs to be a gangster, a would-be author from Kansas, a gay phone sex operator who claims he's straight, a group of rich twentysomethings playing a deadly game of life and death, a vicious Mafia boss, and a sleazy Hollywood movie director. As each of their stories intersect, the body count piles up and the action comes nonstop in this tense, white-knuckle thriller by first-time author Andy Rausch.

"A wild ride. If you like it gangster, *Mad World* delivers."
—Daniel Birch, author of *Get Some*

Burning Bulb
PUBLISHING

BLOODLETTING: A TALE OF REVENGE BY ANDY RAUSCH

"Relentless… Addictive… The kind of nightmare you don't want
to wake up from."
—Heywood Gould, screenwriter of *Rolling Thunder*

He was just an average Joe. But when he finds his family held at
gunpoint by merciless thugs, he's told he must murder a Mafia
chieftain if he ever wishes to see his loved ones again.

Against all odds, Joe keeps his end of the bargain, but the criminals
don't. Now at his wits end, Joe is pushed beyond his breaking point
and forced to exact bloody revenge against those who've done him
and his family wrong in this powerful and violent novella by author
Andy Rausch (*Mad World*).

"Andy Rausch has a tight noir style that combines gritty, realistic drama
with a cinematic flair that makes for a powerful, compelling (somewhat
Stephen Kingesque), authentically visual reading experience."
—Stephen Spignesi, author of *Dialogues*

Burning Bulb
PUBLISHING

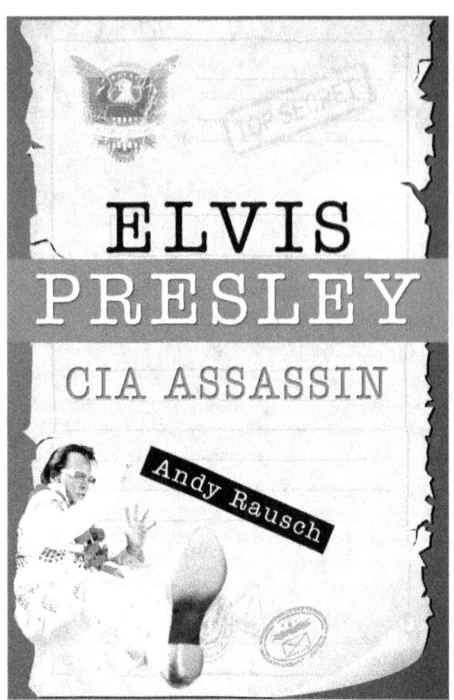

ELVIS PRESLEY, CIA ASSASSIN BY ANDY RAUSCH

"I can guarantee you. Read this book and you'll never look at Elvis the same way again!"
~ Douglas Brode, author of ELVIS CINEMA AND POPULAR CULTURE

SOON TO BE A MAJOR MOTION PICTURE

In 1970, singer Elvis Presley secretly met with President Richard Nixon. This new comedic novel imagines that Presley became a Central Intelligence Agency operative, eventually moving up through the ranks to become a skilled assassin.

Presented in an oral history fashion, the book tells us about Presley's secret transformation by the people who knew him best.

Did he fake his death in 1977? Was Presley involved with the Watergate scandal? The Iran hostage crisis? Communicating with aliens?

Read this book to find out the answers to these and many more questions.

Burning Bulb
PUBLISHING

OTHER GREAT TITLES FROM

WWW.BURNINGBULBPUBLISHING.COM

ANTHOLOGIES
BIZARRO AND TRANSGRESSIVE FICTION

THE BIG BOOK OF BIZARRO

The Big Book of Bizarro brings together the peculiar prose of an international cast of the most grotesquely-gonzo, genre-grinding modern writers who ever put pen to paper (or mouse to pad), including:

NIGHT OF THE LIVING DEAD *horror writers John Russo & George Kosana;* HUSTLER MAGAZINE *erotica contributors Eva Hore, Andrée Lachapelle, & J. Troy Seate and established Bizarro genre authors D. Harlan Wilson, William Pauley III, Wol-vriey, Laird Long, Richard Godwin and so many more!*

From Alien abductions to Zombie sex, The Big Book of Bizarro contains OVER FIFTY STORIES of the most outrélandish transgressive fiction that you'll ever lay your capricious and curious hands upon!

WARNING: This book may be one of the most controversial and dangerous books you'll ever read.

WESTWARD HOES

Nine outlaw writers rode into town from obscurity to pen nine tantalizing tales of horror and fantasy, and leaving once they branded their own personal marks on the weird western genre and became living legends of the American Frontier experience.

Like drunken Indian scouts, the writers fervidly tracked down and captured the Western genre, tore off its fashionable veneer and ravished its exposed essence.

So belly up to the bar with your favorite soiled dove and enjoy perusing these thrilling tales of Old West debauchery, danger and desire; compiled by the publisher of The Big Book of Bizarro and featuring the bizarro novella *Big Trouble in Little Ass* by Wol-vriey.

Burning Bulb
PUBLISHING

ANTHOLOGIES
BIZARRO AND TRANSGRESSIVE FICTION

THE BIG BOOK OF BIZARRO SPECIAL KINDLE EDITIONS

OTHER AWESOME COLLECTIONS

Burning Bulb
PUBLISHING

GARY LEE VINCENT'S
DARKENED
THE WEST VIRGINIA VAMPIRE SERIES

DARKENED HILLS

When evil descends on a small West Virginia town, who will survive?

Jonathan did not start out his life to become a rambler, it just worked out that way. William was a troubled youth with something to hide. Both were from Melas, a small town tucked away in the West Virginia hills... a town where disappearances are happening more and more frequently.

After the suicide of a wanted serial killer, the townsfolk thought the nightmare was over. But when a centuries-old vampire is discovered they find out the hard way it's just getting started. Dark secrets can only stay hidden for so long and when the devil comes to collect, there will be hell to pay. Can Jonathan and William find a way to stop the vampire before it's too late? Find out in *Darkened Hills!*

DARKENED HOLLOWS

In the heart-stopping sequel to the award-winning *Darkened Hills*, Jonathan and William must return to West Virginia to face possible criminal charges stemming from their last visit to the damned town of Melas, where both had narrowly escaped the clutches of a vampire seethe.

And as livestock start mysteriously getting murdered with all of their blood drained, worried farmers are searching for answers - leaving the local Sheriff and his deputy racing against time to learn the cause before a more violent crime is committed.

Burning Bulb
PUBLISHING

WWW.DARKENEDHILLS.COM

GARY LEE VINCENT'S
DARKENED
THE WEST VIRGINIA VAMPIRE SERIES

DARKENED WATERS

When the world goes to hell, the chosen must arise!

As Talman Cane orchestrates a flood of epic proportions in this third installment of the *Darkened* series the towns of Melas and Tarklin are caught completely off guard by the deluge. Hell-bent on finishing what they started, the evil brothers return to the lunatic asylum to take care of the witnesses and add to the ever-growing army of the undead.

Aided by Lucifer himself and the insane vampire demon Legion, the stage is set to channel all of the forces of hell to come forth. In an all-out race to survive, Jonathan, William, and Amanda soon discover they are up against impossible odds as Lucifer opens the Gateway to Hell, ushering in the zombie apocalypse and the End Times.

DARKENED SOULS

Melas and the Madison House are about to be rebuilt.
True evil is about to be reborne!

Young ex-priest and vampire-killer William is drawn back to the West Virginian town that almost killed him, where his vampire arch-enemy Victor Rothenstein still stalks the earth.

The town of Melas lies destroyed after the battle of the End of Days. But why is wealthy Jackie Nixon so eager to rebuild it using the bone dust of murdered souls?

Terrible evil has visited before, but the Gateway to Hell is about to be reopened in a horrific climax. And this time – it's personal.

WWW.DARKENEDHILLS.COM

Burning Bulb
PUBLISHING

WEST VIRGINIA-THEMED HUMORROROTICA
BY RICH BOTTLES JR.

HELLHOLE WEST VIRGINIA

From the heights of Mothman's perch high atop the Silver Bridge in Point Pleasant to the depths of Hellhole Cavern in Pendleton County, evil lurks within the shadows as the sun sets upon the haunted hills and hollows of West Virginia.

Bizarro author Rich Bottles Jr. blows the coffin lid off horror genre clichés with this tour de force cast of Eco-friendly vampires, beach-yearning zombies and sex-starved she-devils.

LUMBERJACKED

If you are easily offended or do not possess a truly depraved sense of humor, this story may not be the light summer reading fare you desire. As for the four feisty female freshmen stranded on top of West Virginia's third highest mountain, they have no choice but to experience the sick, twisted debauchery and perverted mayhem described deep inside the tight unbroken bindings of this horrific missive.

Lumberjacked takes the reader to a nightmarish world where character development and aesthetic integrity are prematurely cut short by the swinging axes of maniacal lumberjacks, who are hell bent on death and destruction in the remote forests of Appalachia. And at the climax, when paranoia crosses over to the paranormal, Lumberjacked makes Deliverance look like a family raft trip down the Lower Gauley.

THE MANACLED

What happens when twin brothers lease out the former West Virginia State Penitentiary with the false purpose of filming a documentary on supernatural phenomena, but their true intention is to make a pornographic movie?

Chaos ensues as the disturbed spirits of murdered convicts, along with the reanimated dead from the neighboring Indian Burial Mound, take their vengeance on the unwary and undressed trespassers.

Zombies, ghosts, mobsters and porn collide in this bizarro tale from horror author Rich Bottles Jr.

Burning Bulb
PUBLISHING

WOL-VRIEY
BIZARRO AND TRANSGRESSIVE FICTION

Burning Bulb
PUBLISHING

BOSTON POSH

In 2028 AD, the USA is a nation ravaged by hungry dragons and dinosaurs. In Boston, Massachusetts, private eye Bud Malone is hired to rescue a kidnapped heiress. But nothing is as it seems. Malone works to unravel a tangled web involving Boston China-town, a 200-year-old woman with a 9-year-old body, white robots, a human-liver-eating psychopath, a golem, a porcelain dragon, and a snake goddess with a crush on him. There's also a woman obsessed with chicken sex. Then Malone meets Posh Lane, a gorgeous call girl who's desperate to quit her pimp. Romantic sparks ignite be-tween Posh and Malone, but Posh's past suddenly catches up with her in a BIG way. To save Posh, Malone agrees to run a quest for Earth's new rulers, the Forks. But, Malone has no idea that agree-ing to the Fork's odd request will send him on the weirdest trip he's ever been on in his life.

VEGAN VAMPIRE VAGINAS

The biggest bank heist in US history. And Tom Palmer can't remember pulling it off. And no, this isn't your standard case of amnesia. After a one-night-stand gone horribly wrong, Boston salesman Tom Palmer wakes up with a vagina implanted in his left hand. Then his day gets worse:

Tom is transported across space-time to a nightmare version of Boston, one where the Bizarro virus has transformed half the population into cannibals. Worst of all, Tom discovers that in this new Boston, he's the infamous gangster Pussypalm, wanted for robbing the Federal Reserve Bank of Boston a year ago. He also learns that the vagina in his hand is prophetic, i.e. it talks . . . after sex. With 130 people left dead during his bank heist and six billion dollars missing, Tom knows he's living on borrowed time. It is in his best interests not to remember anything. Because once he does . . .

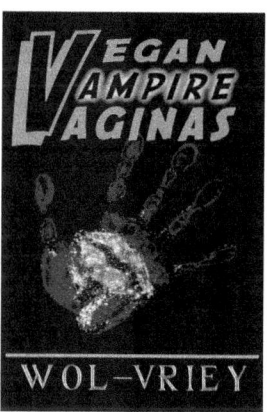

VEGAN ZOMBIE APOCALYPSE

In the post-apocalypse worlderness, zombies rule the earth. They're allergic to meat, and brains literally make them explode. Zombies now eat blood potatoes, parasitic tubers grown in the flesh of humancows corralled in maximum security farms. Two fugitives meet in the ancient ruins of Texas. The first is Soil 15-f, a womancow who's escaped her farm a week before she's due to be killed and her blood potato crop harvested. The second fugitive is Able Kane, former head necros food technician, now sentenced to death for heresy. But Soil is no ordinary humancow. Unknown to herself, she's the vegan zombie agricultural revolution, and the zombies desperately want her back. And the necros equally desper-ately want Able Kane dead. He's fled with a forbidden discovery which will reshape the world for the worse if used. And Able is just hardheaded/misguided enough to use it.

THE FALL OF TOMORROW

Hopelessness... How do you protect your loved ones when Hell itself opens its insidious mouth?
Horror... Nightmarish Creatures invade your world and there is nowhere to hide.
Blood... How long can you hold out before they come for you?
Pain... Where do you run to avoid being eaten alive by monsters with a voracious appetite for your flesh?
Screams... While you selfishly run for your own life.
Questions... Who is to blame? Where did they come from? How many people survived...and how does the human race find the means to fight back?

THE FALL OF TOMORROW is man's last tale of desperation told by those that are striving to salvage some hope against a ravenous bastion of evil beasts bent on ruling our world.

"David Fairhead writes compelling stories that offer very human characters and very inhuman monsters. There is no subtlety in Fairhead's imagination - he is simply dying to scare the hell out of you."
    - Nelson W Pyles - author of DEMONS, DOLLS AND MILKSHAKES

Burning Bulb
PUBLISHING

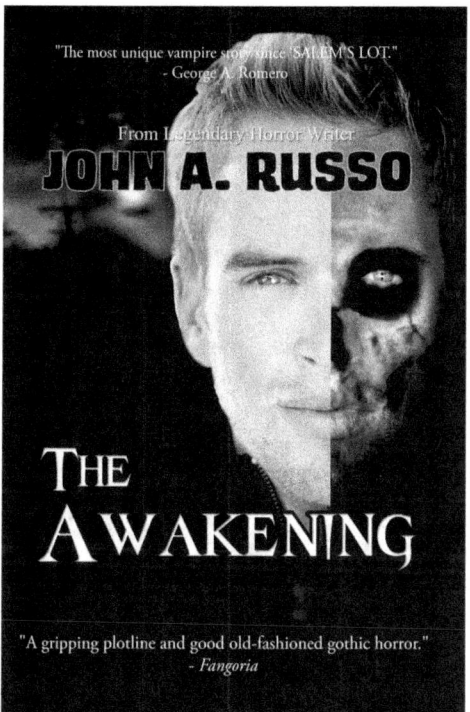

"The most unique vampire story since 'SALEM'S LOT."
- George A. Romero

From Legendary Horror Writer
JOHN A. RUSSO

THE AWAKENING

"A gripping plotline and good old-fashioned gothic horror."
- *Fangoria*

THE AWAKENING

For two hundred years, he has rested. Now he rises. Now he will be satisfied. Nothing can stop him. No one can resist him.

Benjamin Latham is young and handsome, his eighteenth-century mind wakened to a bizarre twentieth-century world. And there is the need deep within . . . an animal need, frightening, murderous, unholy . . . a vital need that must be fed.

And with his need comes a power over men and women to do his bidding, to quiet his dark craving . . .

Until the murders begin. And the inquiries. All suggesting the same hideous truth.

Now Benjamin must find a sanctuary: a lover, a partner, a friend. Someone who can share his darkness. Someone he can lead to . . . The Awakening.

www.TheJohnRusso.com

Burning Bulb
PUBLISHING

Bright little children, at school and at play,
until their minds are stolen away...

A Novel of Terror by
JOHN A. RUSSO
THE
ACADEMY

THE ACADEMY

The Academy. It's every parent's dream, turning their little darlings into geniuses, superachievers, perfect little children.

And if there's a problem, the Academy fixes that too. It's a simple operation. Just a little device. Then a teeny pink scar on a tender little skull . . .

One boy knows the secret. Now he wants his mind back. But it's much, much too late. Too late for anything but the ugly feelings. The bad feelings. The messy sexy feelings. The knife-cold hatred, the murderous rage, for total, screaming, blood-drenching revenge . . .

www.TheJohnRusso.com

Burning Bulb
PUBLISHING

DEALEY PLAZA

From legendary horror and suspense writer JOHN RUSSO comes a harrowing tale where no one is safe!

Dealey Plaza is one of the most notorious places in America, and when youthful conspiracy buffs go there in 1964 to stage their own reenactment of the Kennedy Assassination, four of them are brutally murdered ~ the first victims of a hate-filled legacy that continues for four more decades.

The survivors of that long-ago Dallas trip, each of them now icons of the American way of life, are about to be honored ~ or killed.

Who will live and who will die? Will it be country-western star Lori McCoy? Her loving husband? Her scheming ex-husband? Or the case-hardened FBI agent and longtime friend who risks his life trying to protect them?

www.DealeyPlazaBook.com

Burning Bulb
PUBLISHING

THE MOST FRIGHTENING MOVIE
EVER MADE IS NOW A NOVEL!

NIGHT OF THE LIVING DEAD

Why does **Night of the Living Dead** hit with such chilling impact?
Is it because everyday people in a commonplace house are suddenly the
victims of a monstrous invasion? Or is it because the ghouls who surround
the house with grasping claws were once ordinary people, too?

Decide for yourself as you read, and the horror grips you. All the
cannibalism, suspense and frenzy of the smash-hit move are here in the
novel.

www.TheJohnRusso.com

Burning Bulb
PUBLISHING